## They were almost twenty yards away when the grenade went off

The concussive wave washed over them, and shrapnel cut the foliage from the trees. Sirens screamed across the park, and NOPD patrol cars roared out onto the battlefield.

Ayshe stared at Bolan. "You're not an FBI agent, are you?"

"No, just someone involved in justice," Bolan replied.

"What happens now?" Ayshe asked him.

"I walk away."

"What if I don't let you?" She waggled her pistol at him.

Bolan started to walk away. "Then you get to shoot me in the back," he said over his shoulder.

"Dammit, come back here."

Bolan stopped, then turned and looked at her. "These people have to be stopped, and the police aren't going to be able to do it with their methods. I can. But part of this leads out into the bayou." He paused. "I need a guide, and you were born in the area." He watched her digest his suggestion.

"Do you think you have a lead on these people?" she finally asked.

"Yeah, and it starts with Papa Glapion. But he's not the guy handling the organ brokering. Someone else has the connections."

# MACK BOLAN ®

## The Executioner

#152 Combat Stretch
#153 Firebase Florida
#154 Night Hit
#155 Hawaiian Heat
#156 Phantom Force
#157 Cayman Strike
#158 Firing Line
#159 Steel and Flame
#160 Storm Warning
#161 Eye of the Storm
#162 Colors of Hell
#163 Warrior's Edge
#164 Death Trail
#165 Fire Sweep
#166 Assassin's Creed
#167 Double Action
#168 Blood Price
#169 White Heat
#170 Baja Blitz
#171 Deadly Force
#172 Fast Strike
#173 Capitol Hit
#174 Battle Plan
#175 Battle Ground
#176 Ransom Run
#177 Evil Code
#178 Black Hand
#179 War Hammer
#180 Force Down
#181 Shifting Target
#182 Lethal Agent
#183 Clean Sweep
#184 Death Warrant
#185 Sudden Fury
#186 Fire Burst
#187 Cleansing Flame

#188 War Paint
#189 Wellfire
#190 Killing Range
#191 Extreme Force
#192 Maximum Impact
#193 Hostile Action
#194 Deadly Contest
#195 Select Fire
#196 Triburst
#197 Armed Force
#198 Shoot Down
#199 Rogue Agent
#200 Crisis Point
#201 Prime Target
#202 Combat Zone
#203 Hard Contact
#204 Rescue Run
#205 Hell Road
#206 Hunting Cry
#207 Freedom Strike
#208 Death Whisper
#209 Asian Crucible
#210 Fire Lash
#211 Steel Claws
#212 Ride the Beast
#213 Blood Harvest

# DON PENDLETON'S
# THE EXECUTIONER®
## BLOOD HARVEST

## A GOLD EAGLE BOOK FROM
# WORLDWIDE.®

TORONTO • NEW YORK • LONDON
AMSTERDAM • PARIS • SYDNEY • HAMBURG
STOCKHOLM • ATHENS • TOKYO • MILAN
MADRID • WARSAW • BUDAPEST • AUCKLAND

First edition September 1996
ISBN 0-373-64213-X

Special thanks and acknowledgment to
Mel Odom for his contribution to this work.

BLOOD HARVEST

No Connections, Interests, or Intercessions...will avail to prevent strict execution of justice.

—George Washington

There is no glory in profiting from the weakness of others. Those who try to take, either by stealth or force, what does not belong to them, will be brought to justice.

—Mack Bolan

# THE
# MACK BOLAN®
## LEGEND

Nothing less than a war could have fashioned the destiny of the man called Mack Bolan. Bolan earned the Executioner title in the jungle hell of Vietnam.

But this soldier also wore another name—Sergeant Mercy. He was so tagged because of the compassion he showed to wounded comrades-in-arms and Vietnamese civilians.

Mack Bolan's second tour of duty ended prematurely when he was given emergency leave to return home and bury his family, victims of the Mob. Then he declared a one-man war against the Mafia.

He confronted the Families head-on from coast to coast, and soon a hope of victory began to appear. But Bolan had broken society's every rule. That same society started gunning for this elusive warrior—to no avail.

So Bolan was offered amnesty to work within the system against terrorism. This time, as an employee of Uncle Sam, Bolan became Colonel John Phoenix. With a command center at Stony Man Farm in Virginia, he and his new allies—Able Team and Phoenix Force—waged relentless war on a new adversary: the KGB.

But when his one true love, April Rose, died at the hands of the Soviet terror machine, Bolan severed all ties with Establishment authority.

Now, after a lengthy lone-wolf struggle and much soul-searching, the Executioner has agreed to enter an "arm's-length" alliance with his government once more, reserving the right to pursue personal missions in his Everlasting War.

# PROLOGUE

*New Orleans, Louisiana*

"Buy a lady a drink?"

Toby Lavek looked up through the haze of blue smoke that had settled over the interior of the Frog Pond Bar & Grill and saw her reflected in the mirror behind the bar.

She was easily the most gorgeous woman in the place. A turquoise minidress clung to her every curve. Even in the dim light, her deep tan glowed, contrasting dramatically with her punk-cut tawny blond hair.

"Do you always take this long to make up your mind?" the blonde asked, her smoky voice slow and teasing.

"Not usually," Lavek replied. So far, he'd been approached by three hookers, a pair of women from out of town looking for a good time and a couple of Cajun fishermen who thought he was someone they knew.

After the kind of day he'd had, the tavern had seemed the perfect place to escape to. Lavek figured nobody would know him there, and the clientele were not the sort to talk politics.

"Did you have a bad day?" the woman asked. Her voice held the trace of an accent, but Lavek couldn't quite place it. New Orleans was a melting pot of dialects and cultures. Lavek had lived there for the last seven years, long enough to be certain she wasn't native to New Orleans, or even to America.

He smiled. "Job lag." He gestured to the stool beside him. "What would you like to drink?"

"A beer would be fine."

Lavek caught the bartender's attention, pointed to his bottle, then held up two fingers. The man retrieved two beers from the fridge, uncapped them and set them on the bar. Lavek paid.

When the woman drank, she did so with gusto. Her throat muscles worked smoothly, and when she set the beer back on the bar, fully a third of it was gone. "Job lag," she said, her eyes bright. "That was a joke."

Lavek felt as though he was watching an exotic feline: playful, but with sharp claws.

"What do you do?" she asked.

"I'm involved in politics," he answered.

"I'm sure you're successful," she said. "You're a very handsome man."

Although only twenty-seven years old, Lavek had been in the political arena long enough to have learned that nothing was given free—not even a compliment. He wondered what the woman's angle was.

"Thank you," he said shortly.

She smiled. "You think I'm kidding. But it's really who we are inside that counts, don't you agree? My name's Kaliope, by the way."

Lavek introduced himself. For the first time in the dim light he noticed that her eyes were a mismatched aquamarine and brown, creating an effect that was almost hypnotic. The conversation flowed easily between them, and Lavek found himself becoming so engrossed in her that he didn't even notice the time passing.

"I live not far from here," Kaliope said finally. "I think we could both do with some coffee."

Lavek nodded, and they left the bar. The air hung hot and heavy. She continued talking as they walked along. The beers Lavek had consumed, combined with his heavy work load of the last few weeks, lowered whatever inhibitions he might have had, and he found himself flirting easily with her.

Kaliope turned into a narrow stairway, and Lavek followed her up to a second-floor apartment. Moonlight flooded through the windows, and he thought she looked even more alluring cloaked in the shadows.

Without bothering to turn on a light, she turned toward Lavek and wrapped her arms around him as her mouth sought his.

He tasted her breath, sweetly alcoholic, and felt her tongue against his. He dropped his hand to the softness of her breast.

"You must be some kind of siren," Lavek said when they drew apart. "I can't remember when I felt this out of control."

Kaliope smiled. "I'm glad you're enjoying it."

Lavek was about to pick up where they'd left off, when he felt a short, stabbing pain in the back of his neck. He turned. Two men stood behind him. Something silver and sharp glinted in the hands of one of them.

"Okay," a man's voice said. "He's done."

Lavek's mind began to spin and his vision blurred. He tried to reach for Kaliope and saw her watching him with detachment before he fell. Then everything went black.

WHEN LAVEK CAME TO, it was morning. His tongue felt thick in his dry mouth, and he struggled to focus. The first thing he noticed were the uniformed policemen in the room. Then he saw the blood.

There was a lot of it, and it had stained the white sheets on the bed.

"Christ," he heard a grizzled sergeant say. "The son of a bitch who did this should be taken out and shot."

"It's those goddamned Haitians slipping into the country," another man growled. Lavek noticed that the cop was working on a pair of handcuffs that held him to the wrought-iron bedpost. "This makes fourteen cases that I know of."

"Nineteen," a third cop said. "And it's not the Haitians. It's those voodoo people. What'd they take, Frank?"

The first cop knelt over Lavek, who followed his gaze, a strangled cry escaping his lips. A huge gash covered in coagulated blood ran along his right side.

"Looks like maybe a kidney," the cop said. "If they'd taken anything else, he'd be dead now." He met Lavek's terrified eyes. "Take it easy, son. You're going to be okay. An ambulance is on its way."

"Jesus," one of the other cops said as he went through Lavek's pants. Lavek could see that they had been cut off him. "This guy is Harris Mercury's stepson. He was reported missing two days ago."

Two days. The statement sent Lavek's mind reeling. He wanted to cry out, but he felt too weak to do so. He was barely aware of the bedroom door opening to admit the medical team before he gratefully lost consciousness.

**1**

Mack Bolan, a.k.a. the Executioner, stood hidden in the shadows of the New Orleans Marina, his compact night glasses trained on the sleek yacht that was motoring toward the lakefront.

He knew the crew aboard the *Silver Kestrel* was finishing its current project. Since Hal Brognola had asked him to take a look at developments in New Orleans, the Executioner had taken less than twenty hours to turn up a leverage point. That point was Eduard Hamlin, one of the city's largest black-market dealers. The *Silver Kestrel*, though it could never be proved on paper, belonged to Hamlin.

Putting the night glasses away, Bolan started toward the lakefront.

He walked to the end of the pier, where a man was tying up the yacht. The boat's deck was empty, although soft yellow lights emanated from the two forward ports and the companionway.

The guy looked up at Bolan's approach. "Can I do something for you, buddy?" he asked. Tall and thickset, he wore a beard, and a gold hoop pierced his left ear. He took the cigarette that hung from his lips and flicked it out into the water. His right hand drifted near the bulge on his hip under his windbreaker.

"I need to see the captain," Bolan said with an easy smile.

"He's busy," the guy replied.

Bolan moved closer, cutting the distance between them. "It won't take a minute." With combat senses searching the darkness around them, the soldier felt certain that he was being watched.

"You don't hear so well," the man said, drawing a Colt 10 mm pistol from the holster on his hip. "Back off, or you're going to get hurt."

In a blur of movement, Bolan pulled out the PR-24 police billy club from beneath his black duster and swept it in a short arc that connected with the hardman's gun wrist.

The pistol went spinning away. The man backpedaled and tried to escape his attacker, his mouth opening to scream a warning as he held on to his broken wrist.

Bolan slashed the PR-24 against the man's temple, cutting off his scream. The guy fell heavily, rendered unconscious by the blow.

Suddenly a shot split the air, the bullet tearing splinters from the dock post near the Executioner's head. Bolan ran toward the yacht, leaped the gap between the dock and the boat, cushioning himself in a roll that brought him up against the vessel's cabin. Rising, he unlimbered the silenced Beretta 93-R from its shoulder leather.

Another bullet ripped into the coaming of the yacht, giving Bolan a fix on the shooter's position.

With the Beretta gripped in both hands, he found the shooter. The guy was taking cover behind a small shed on the shoreline. The guy fired another pair of shots that made the life preserver on the cabin wall behind Bolan jump.

Bolan squeezed the trigger, drilling a round into the shooter's exposed shoulder. The impact caused the gunman to jerk out from behind the shed, and the Executioner followed up with a pair of bullets that hit the center of his target's chest. The man slumped forward, dead before he hit the ground.

Three men surfaced from belowdecks at the aft end of the yacht, all bristling guns. One of the gunners shone a beam of light over the dock.

Bolan took out the guy with the flashlight first, putting four shots into the man's upper body, driving him backward over the gunwale.

The other two men dived for cover.

From the brief glimpse Bolan had gotten of the men, he thought they'd looked Eastern European. The intel he'd been given was that buyers were in New Orleans looking for computer chips. Eduard Hamlin's black-market lines provided a multitude of things, including technological secrets, if the price was right.

Bolan edged forward, the pistol held level in both hands.

"There he is!" one of the men yelled in Russian, breaking from cover.

As he brought his gun around, Bolan fired. All three parabellum rounds took the man in the face, and he crumpled to the deck. The Executioner reacted to the sweep of the mini-Uzi in the other guy's fist by vaulting into the lifeboat to his right. A burst of 9 mm rounds chopped into the deck and the lifeboat, searching for their target.

Bolan covered the length of the lifeboat in two long strides. At the stern of the small boat, he placed his free hand on the gunwale, then swung both legs toward the hardman. His feet connected solidly with his adversary at chest height and the guy went overboard, his weapon firing harmlessly into the sky.

The soldier leaped onto the deck and moved toward the companionway. He turned the corner in time to spot another man standing in the shadowed recess, holding a pistol. Before the guy could react, the Executioner slammed the butt of the Beretta into his face. Blood spurted from his broken nose as the man tumbled down the short flight of stairs, unconscious.

Bolan hurried down the steps into the galley below, where two men were frantically working along the bulkhead, trying to secure a hidden hatch behind the short sofa.

One of them spun to face him, bringing up a .45.

The soldier didn't hesitate. He stroked the Beretta's trigger and hit the third button on his adversary's silk shirt. A dark red rose blossomed on the material. The man sprawled backward, coming to a rest against a small stove built into the bulkhead.

Covering the other guy, the Executioner said, "He made his last mistake. You don't have to."

The gunner held up his hands. "Are you a cop?"

"No. What's in the compartment?"

"Money."

"Hamlin's?"

"Yeah."

"Get it." Bolan glanced around as the guy on the floor began to stir, shifting the Beretta to follow his line of vision.

"Over on your face," Bolan commanded him. "Hands behind your head."

The man complied, blood running down his face from the gash on his forehead.

The guy in the silk shirt took a navy duffel bag from the hidden compartment.

"You have a gun?" Bolan asked.

The crewman nodded.

"Throw it out the porthole."

Without a word, he did as the Executioner commanded.

After relieving the corpse and his other prisoner of their weapons, Bolan walked to the stove and turned on all the burners. The sickly sweet smell of propane gas began to fill the galley.

Bolan knew that taking Hamlin's money and killing a few of his customers would only inconvenience Hamlin, but destroying his yacht and focusing the attention of the New Orleans Police Department on Hamlin would really hurt him. He took a block of plastic explosive he'd already prepped with a remote-control detonator from his duster pocket and tossed it next to the stove. The propane was beginning to make breathing difficult.

"Let's go," the Executioner ordered the two men. He slung the duffel bag over his shoulder, as the guy with the broken nose led the way.

Above deck, Bolan gestured over the side of the yacht. "Dive deep and swim hard," he advised them.

After they'd jumped, he settled the duffel bag more securely over his shoulder, then shook the empty magazine from his pistol and reloaded it.

A helicopter thundered overhead, a searchlight mounted under its belly sweeping over the black water around the yacht.

Bolan looked at the pier, which rose above him at a distance of eight feet. After making sure it was deserted, he holstered the 93-R and jumped, his fingers catching the edge as the chopper's searchlight swept over him. The aircraft dropped low enough for him to see the two men inside the Plexiglas bubble.

His muscles beginning to take strain, Bolan threw a leg over the edge of the pier and rolled up onto it. Without getting up, he palmed the 9 mm pistol and fired four warning shots. Two of them ricocheted off the aircraft's skids.

The chopper pilot immediately pulled his craft up and veered away.

Bolan took off running. At the same time, he removed the detonator from his pocket, flipped back the protective cover and depressed the button. A heartbeat later, the yacht blew up, the yellow-blue flames of the igniting propane gas lighting the sky.

By the time the soldier reached the end of the pier, the initial fever of the fire had burned itself out. The Executioner melted into the night.

BOLAN DROVE along Pontchartrain Boulevard toward the I-610 cloverleaf. From his quick look at the money in the duffel bag, he could tell the amount was considerable. He was certain Hamlin would know about the attack by now, and he was equally certain police officials would soon be chatting with the black marketer.

The ebony Dodge Stealth R/T Turbo handled well, and Bolan enjoyed its responsiveness. With its all-wheel drive and steer and 320-horsepower, the Stealth guaranteed performance and maneuverability, especially useful with all the out-of-town traffic flooding the city for Mardi Gras.

After getting the call from Brognola, Bolan had arranged for the car and sent in the equipment stats. Aaron Kurtzman, Stony Man Farm's cybernetics specialist, was working out the new ownership papers as well as the Executioner's cover ID.

A glance at the cellular phone-answering machine combo on the passenger side of the car showed that someone had logged on a message. He punched the Play button.

"Mr. Fox, this is Della Nicks at Specialty Courier. We have your package waiting for you." This was followed by directions to the building and a phone number.

Bolan copied the information in his warbook. A brief check on the map showed him the courier service was only a few blocks from the NOPD's main headquarters. There'd be time to pick up the package later. Shooting through the cloverleaf, he took the elevated highway, then the on ramp to I-10.

He punched the Send button on the cellular phone, then keyed in the nonemergency number for the police department. It rang twice before being answered.

Bolan used the clip-on mike on the sun visor above his head, leaving his hands free. "This is Agent Fox of the FBI. Can you connect me with someone in Homicide?"

"A moment, sir."

While he waited, Bolan briefly studied the city map again. His intel had also included a rundown on the after-hours clubs around the city, naming two that Hamlin owned. The clubs were illegal, opening up after licensed establishments had closed for the night and staying open until the early-morning hours.

The entertainment in some of them was often highly sexual, and the profits were enormous. From what Bolan had pieced together, Hamlin put a percentage of his black-market monies into the clubs, added other profits, then made most of it legal tender again through stock portfolios and investment certificates.

"Lockspur," a raspy male voice announced.

"This is Special Agent Fox of the FBI," Bolan said, quickly flipping through the pages of the warbook until he reached his intel on the NOPD. Apparently Lockspur was a captain in the police force.

"What can I do for you?" Lockspur asked.

Bolan knew the cop wasn't going to like what he had to say. "Actually it's what I can do for you."

"And what's that?"

"For the next week or so, I'm going to be attached to your department."

"Homicide?"

"Right." Bolan changed lanes and blew by an eighteen-wheeler.

"Regarding what?" Lockspur's tone was cautious.

"The investigations your teams have been making under the code name Carrion Killings." Bolan knew using the unofficial designation the NOPD detectives had been whispering among themselves would get Lockspur's attention. The media hadn't picked up on it yet. Kurtzman had hacked his way into the NOPD's computer systems and pulled actual field reports.

"I think you're out of your jurisdiction," Lockspur said. "Those investigations are purely domestic. There's nothing federal about them."

"That started to change when Harris Mercury's stepson ended up missing a kidney in a French Quarter hotel three days ago," Bolan said. "The lock came yesterday, when a heart turned up in Atlanta, Georgia, that could possibly belong to a Chalina Rodriguiz."

There was a pause, and Bolan could hear the clatter of a computer keyboard in the background. "She was one of ours," Lockspur said. "She was killed nine days ago."

"Right," Bolan replied. He took the exit road. "A DNA test IDed the heart as probably belonging to her. And that means the felons have crossed state lines."

"You've come a long way on a *probably*," Lockspur said.

"I'm also here because Senator Harris Mercury has considerable pull up on the Hill."

"If it was the Rodriguiz woman's heart," the homicide cop said, "what was it doing in Atlanta?"

"That's part of what I'm here to find out." Bolan turned east. The after-hours club was only a few blocks away. "The popular theory that the murders are being committed because of American involvement in Haiti isn't holding water with Mercury. He wants to know who nearly killed his stepson."

"And you're the guy with all the answers," Lockspur growled.

"No," Bolan told him, "I'm just an extra hand. I won't be in the way, but I need access to your records."

"Get me something in writing that I can show my chain of command."

"You'll get a fax at seven o'clock." He glanced at his watch. It was 3:45 a.m. "I'll need to meet with you some time this morning."

"Are you in the city?" Lockspur asked.

"Yeah."

"What hotel?"

Bolan grinned, knowing the man intended to have him checked out and placed under surveillance. "I haven't found one yet."

"I take it you're not hanging out at the bus station."

"No."

Once it became clear Bolan wasn't going to volunteer any information, Lockspur went on. "Can you be here by eight-thirty?"

"Sure."

"I'll be there." He broke the connection, then punched in another number. This one barely rang before it was picked up.

"Hamlin." The voice was deep and smooth.

"Who's been killing people and stealing their organs in New Orleans?" Bolan asked.

"Who is this?" Hamlin demanded.

"I'm the guy who sunk your boat," the Executioner answered. "Who's behind the vivisection slayings in this city?"

"I don't know what you're talking about," Hamlin said.

"Too bad. Your ignorance is going to cost you more than just the *Silver Kestrel*." He punched the End button.

THE AFTER-HOURS CLUB was tucked between two old buildings surrounded by rusty wrought-iron railings, and no signs advertised the club's presence. The patrons found out about it through word of mouth.

Bolan parked his vehicle in an alley four blocks away. He dropped the Beretta in the trunk and added the false ID he'd been traveling under. He picked up the cellular phone, and pager from a canvas bag. The phone went into a pocket of the duster, and the pager he clipped to his belt.

A buzzer was mounted in the brick wall beside the club's entrance. He tried the door anyway and found it locked. He pressed the buzzer, giving it two good short taps, then stepped back.

"Yeah?" The door swung outward slightly, revealing a heavyset man wearing a dark suit that did little to conceal his muscles.

"I was told I could get a drink here," Bolan said, holding out a hundred-dollar bill.

"Somebody told you wrong."

Bolan grinned and left the hundred hanging. "You're a security guard. You're not wearing the suit to watch empty buildings."

"Give me a name."

"Revis Benoit." The name belonged to a guy the after-hours club hired to pass along the word for them. According to Bolan's information, Benoit was a street grifter with a past record.

"Where'd you meet Benoit?"

"In Pat O'Brien's a few weeks back."

The bouncer took the bill. "Okay. Inside."

Bolan stepped into the dimly lit foyer. It was empty except for a security camera mounted in the far corner over a metal door that looked like it could withstand an antitank gun attack.

"Get up against the wall and spread 'em," the bouncer said.

Bolan assumed the position. The man searched him, turning up the pager and the cellular phone, which he held in his beefy hands.

"You got any ID?" the big man asked.

"I got relieved of it a few months ago," Bolan answered. "I've been meaning to get a library card."

"Weapons?" the bouncer asked as he stepped away.

"Not on me," Bolan replied. "I'd like my phone and pager back now."

The bouncer glanced at them but didn't return them.

"It's business. I'm expecting a call, and I'd like to have a couple of drinks while I wait."

"What kind of business?"

"I move things around."

"You know who Joey Ziff is?" the bouncer asked, testing him.

"Sure. He makes book over in the Vieux Carre. But he doesn't like to deal with the big guys," Bolan replied, having done his homework.

The bouncer smiled slightly. "That's Joey. If he had more guts, he'd have more bucks." He handed the phone back to Bolan, but held on to the pager. "You got this as well as the phone?" He tossed it into the air and caught it.

"I do some business on the side," Bolan said. "The guys I work for buy my time, but they don't buy all of it. A man working his own hook shouldn't put all his eggs in one basket."

"Right." The bouncer flipped the pager at him.

Bolan caught it and clipped it onto his waistband.

"You're clean for weapons and wires," the bouncer said. "But if you've got any drugs, keep them to yourself. The management's already leased out the franchise in that department." He pressed the buzzer next to the metal door. "Wicked Wanda's got the stage tonight."

Bolan opened the heavy door, then climbed a dark, narrow flight of stairs to a second door, which opened at his touch.

Two more bouncers were at this station. They nodded to Bolan, and he followed a scantily clad cocktail waitress to a small round table for two in a corner. She assured him he'd be able to see the show just fine, and dimpled when he dropped a tip on her tray and ordered a drink.

Bolan looked around. The floor space in the club was small. Dark curtains covered black-painted windows. Most of the tables were for two-to-four guests, with some of them pushed together to provide seating for a larger group.

The soldier estimated that more than two hundred people were in the club. Three bartenders handled the drinks from behind an L-shaped bar jutting into the room. Chrome and mirrors barely captured reflections in the dim light, blunted even further by the cloud of smoke that hung over the room.

The waitress returned with his drink. She was young and blond, her long hair reaching to her narrow waist. She placed the drink on the table in front of him.

"Is there a phone?" Bolan asked.

"In the back," she replied, pointing.

Bolan folded a bill and stuffed it in her tip glass. "Thanks." He made his way across the crowded dance floors where couples moved to the heavy metal rock blasting from the speakers.

Three pay phones were in the back near the bathrooms. Bolan checked for a fire-alarm pull along the way but didn't find one. However, he spotted two more bouncers, marking them in his mind, as he lifted the handset of the first phone. He dialed the number from memory.

It rang eight times before it was picked up by Dennis Wynnewood, counselor-at-law. "This had better be damned good," he barked, his voice thick with sleep.

"I want to talk to you about the heart that turned up in Atlanta," Bolan said.

There was a pause. "Who is this?" Wynnewood demanded.

"A guy who knows you brokered the heart for Spencer Dane." That information had come from Brognola. After the heart had surfaced in Atlanta, FBI agents had quietly probed into Dane, who'd been on a donor waiting list for a heart transplant. The thirty-three-year-old man had been plagued with congestive heart failure most of his adult life, but had the money to afford Wynnewood's exorbitant fees. To Bolan's way of thinking, the only thing Dane had been guilty of was trying to up the odds of getting a donor.

"I don't know what you're talking about." Wynnewood hadn't been approached by the FBI yet. Brognola had sold the Bureau on letting him move onto the scene for a time without their follow-up. Dane had paid Wynnewood in cash, and without a lot of digging, a case couldn't be made.

"You will."

"Look," Wynnewood said, "if this is some kind of shakedown, I'm not falling for it."

"It's not a shakedown, Counselor," the Executioner replied. "I'd be willing to negotiate a plea bargain. But first I want you to see what I have for openers. There's an after-hours club that'll be in today's news. Watch for it.'' Bolan hung up the phone.

Back in the club proper, three women dressed in revealing black leather and fishnet stockings gyrated on the small stage. The dance floor had been cleared, and the audience sat and watched.

Bolan went into the men's room. It had a low paneled ceiling, and the walls were covered with explicit graffiti. Three stalls flanked a row of urinals sunk into the floor. In the one at the end, a pair of wing-tipped shoes vigorously confronted a single high-heeled shoe.

The soldier stepped into the first cubicle, ignoring the sounds coming from the end stall. He unhooked the water-supply tubing and let the water gush onto the floor. Then he removed the tank lid and used it to smash the tank. As more water spilled out onto the floor, the noises from the end stall suddenly quietened, leaving only the sound of running water. Porcelain lay in pieces on the floor.

As Bolan stepped out of the cubicle, he saw a guy emerge from the last stall with a platinum blonde hanging on his arm.

"Shit," the guy said, stuffing his shirt back into his pants, "what happened?"

"The damn thing exploded," Bolan replied.

"Come on," the woman said, pulling at her dress, "let's get out of here."

The man followed her. "I'll let somebody know," he said over his shoulder.

"Do that." Bolan doubted the noise had been heard over the music blasting from the stage. When they'd gone, he removed the cellular phone from his pocket and took it apart. It separated easily into three pieces. Reaching up to the ceiling, he shoved one of the panels aside. Then he flipped the activation toggle on one of the pieces. It beeped. He put it in the hole, then pulled the panel back into place.

Bolan went back into the club, passing one of the bouncers on his way to check out the men's room. On the stage, Wicked Wanda and her cohorts were down to bare flesh.

The bouncer returned from the men's room, his face screwed up in disgust. He made his way over to the bar.

Bolan quickly stashed another part of the cellular phone under his table, the third part going under one of the stools facing the bar.

He slipped the pager from his belt and keyed in the proper sequence until a red light on the readout formed a number 3.

The Executioner noted the bouncer using the phone at the bar, talking excitedly. He placed his thumb on the firing button of the pager—actually a radio detonator—for the two flash-bangs and the one incendiary explosive he'd planted in the club just as the bouncer caught his eye.

**2**

"He's in here."

Marie Desermeaux followed the frantic woman through the candlelit confines of the small cottage situated deep in the bayou. "Everything is going to be all right, *cher,*" she said, her voice gentle. "You did good to call me. I sense the evil here, but I can get rid of it." She clutched a cloth bag containing her medicines and herbs, and willed herself to believe her own words. The evil that clung to the small cottage felt almost palpable to her heightened senses.

"When Didier told me how he found him," the woman said, "I was sure he was dead, laying in the water that way. It's a miracle the gators didn't get him."

The last room in the house contained two double beds. Desermeaux knew at a glance that the parents slept in the same room as their children. The boy's father knelt by the sagging bed where the boy lay, almost lost in the pile of feather pillows and blankets. The only light came from an oil lamp that stood on a scarred chest of drawers.

"This is the woman?" the man asked his wife. He was thin and whipcord tough through exposure to the elements and hard work. His hands were covered in a network of scars from fishing nets and knife blades. Fear filled his eyes.

"I am Marie Desermeaux," she told him. "Let me see the boy." Barely five feet tall, she'd seen a hundred pounds only during her three pregnancies. Her dark skin reflected her mixed roots. After being wakened by the pounding at her door less than thirty minutes earlier, she'd drawn back her long gray hair with a rubber band and thrown a cloak over her simple homespun dress to guard against the chill she so often felt these days.

"You're the witch?" the man asked, reluctantly moving away from the bedside.

"I am the *traiteur.*" She knelt beside the boy, noticing the gray cast of his skin.

"I don't want my boy coming back as a zombie," the man said, his voice catching in his throat. "Better he die and I bury him. Better the gators got him."

"Is Tibob going to be a zombie?" a small voice asked.

Desermeaux turned her head and saw three small girls standing in the doorway. They reminded her of her granddaughter, Marisa, at that age. She glanced at the woman. "Get your man and your babies out of here, *cher*."

The man protested at first, but the woman hustled him out.

Desermeaux pulled the covers back from the boy and looked at him, taking in the almost imperceptible rise and fall of his chest.

His mother returned to the room and stood at the foot of the bed. "Is my boy going to be all right?"

"He's alive," Desermeaux said. "That is a very good thing." She pulled back his eyelid and studied his glassy stare. Laying her fingers on the side of the boy's neck, she felt the thready, uneven pulse.

"My husband, what he said about a zombie..." The woman's voice broke.

"What is your name?"

The woman wiped the tears from her cheeks. "Judithe," she said.

"Before tonight, did you know me?" Desermeaux opened the boy's shirt and looked at the incision that had been made from his ribs down to his hip. At first she was surprised that the boy hadn't died of blood loss, then she realized the cut was only deep enough to gain entry into the body cavity.

"No," Judithe replied.

"And what did you hear about me, *cher?*" Desermeaux reached into her medicine bag and took out a vial. Gently she poured some of the contents into Tibob's mouth. She pinched his nose to make him swallow.

"That you had the gift of healing."

Desermeaux nodded. "And that's all I am. I'm no *bokor* to make the dead rise and become slaves. Your son will not become a zombie by my hand. My gift has nothing to do with voodoo."

Judithe moved forward and knelt beside the older woman. Tears trickled down her face. "My husband, Didier, said he has seen such things. When he was younger, he attended a voodoo ceremony. Not one of those put on for the tourists, but the real thing."

Desermeaux gently touched the incision. Already she could feel the heat of an infection. She dipped back into her bag.

"He said Tibob looks like some of the people he saw at that ceremony," Judithe continued.

"That may be, but this child is no zombie. He has been badly hurt, but we can deal with that." Desermeaux took out a small plastic bag containing crushed grass and began to sprinkle it over the wound.

"What is that?" Judithe asked.

"*La Mauve.* It will help him fight the infection. I'll need some hot water and fresh towels."

The woman went to get them.

While she was gone, Desermeaux took out a string of chinaberries and put them around the boy's neck. They would also help stave off the fever.

When Judithe returned, Desermeaux made a poultice and bandaged the boy's wound as best she could. "Stay with him," she said. "I will call the hospital. He needs more attention than I can give him." She took Judithe's hands in hers. "Be strong, because I know your boy will be all right. I have looked at his palm and seen this. You must believe me."

"I do."

Gathering her cloak around her, Desermeaux walked back through the house, passing Judithe's husband, who sat in a wooden rocker on the screened-in galley with his three daughters.

Desermeaux's old Dodge pickup was parked outside. To the right of the cottage stood a rickety garage built out over the bayou water. It housed the small motorboat Judithe had used to go to Desermeaux's home, then piloted back along the bayou to guide the way.

Climbing into the ancient pickup, Desermeaux slid across the duct-taped seats and lifted the cellular phone her granddaughter had given her. She called 911 first, letting them know that police and an emergency rescue team were needed. Then she called Marisa at home. There was no answer. She hung up and tried her work number.

"Collins, Homicide."

"I need to speak with Marisa Ayshe," Desermeaux said.

"She's not here. But I can get a message to her."

Desermeaux left one, describing the situation. Marisa was part of the team investigating attacks such as the one Tibob had suffered.

It started to rain; and she watched it sluice down the windshield of the pickup. Without warning, the *avartisment*—the vision—swept over her as it had done ever since she could remember. As a child, she'd thought they were nightmares. Then she'd begun to see they were portents of the future.

The face rippled. At first she thought it was because she was seeing it in the rain across the windshield. Then she realized the face was under water, the flesh gray and slack, reminding her of the boy inside the cottage. She knew she was seeing the latest victim of the attacks taking place around the city.

For a moment, she almost had a sense of the *bokor*—the voodoo man—who was behind the attacks. Then it slipped away. Marisa came to her next, her features glistening with perspiration, her dark eyes large with fear. Desermeaux saw the pistol in her granddaughter's hands. She tried to see what it was that threatened her granddaughter, but the vision slipped away from her.

Desermeaux came to, gasping for breath, her heart thudding painfully in her chest. She took her umbrella from behind the seat, climbed shakily out of the pickup and walked back to the cottage.

Marisa was in danger. The boy had to live. He might be able to tell them who had attacked him. Desermeaux knew she would do everything in her power to help him survive.

THE INCENDIARY EXPLOSIVE in the club's men's room blew the door off its hinges. Flames shot out, followed by billowing smoke.

Most of the club's clientele were up out of their chairs and racing for the single door. Still in a state of undress, Wicked Wanda and her playmates scampered from the stage and toward the entrance as well.

For a moment, the bouncer's attention was divided between his phone call and the fiery explosion. Then he reached for the pistol in his shoulder holster and turned to confront Bolan.

Already tracking the movement of the other three bouncers in the club, Bolan swept a heavy pitcher of beer from the bar top and swung it hard. The glass container connected with the man's face, knocking him unconscious to the floor. The Executioner grabbed the gun from the guy's slack fist.

It was a Smith & Wesson SP-2 .40-caliber pistol. Bolan flicked off the safety as he spun to face the other bouncers, but the people fleeing from the club made it impossible to get off a shot without hitting one of them.

The bouncers were less concerned. They fired, their bullets shattering the glass bottles and mirrors behind the bar.

Bolan went low and came up beside a table. He kicked it over and bullets thudded into it, some of them penetrating the thick particle-board.

Tapping the control button on the remote detonator, Bolan brought up the frequency for the second bomb. The resulting flash-bang caught the bouncers off guard. Taking advantage of the moment, Bolan took aim from around his table and fired at the nearest man. The bullet sped true and cored through the man's head, carrying enough impact to knock him off his feet.

The crowd had cleared the room, leaving only Bolan and the two remaining bouncers. The warrior tripped the final flash-bang, larger than the first one, and moved out from behind his table immediately after the detonation. He stood, the S&W SP-2 clasped in both hands.

The last bouncer fired twice, trying for his target with a frenzied desperation.

Without breaking stride, Bolan stroked the trigger. The round caught the man in the throat and knocked him backward over a table. He struggled to bring his weapon around as he started drowning in his own blood. The Executioner fired a mercy round that ended the man's struggle.

Glancing around the burning club, Bolan felt satisfied with his work. He didn't think anything could be salvaged from the club, and setting up another such operation somewhere else would cost Eduard Hamlin a lot of time and money.

Bolan slipped an extra magazine from the jacket pocket of one of the dead bouncers, then headed for the door. He met the doorman coming up.

The guy started to raise his pistol, but the Executioner fired first. The round drilled through the man's right shoulder and knocked him back down the stairs.

The soldier reached the ground floor at almost the same time as the fallen doorman. He pointed his weapon at the guy's head, freezing his attempts to get his dropped pistol.

"Who the hell are you?" the doorman gasped, clutching his wounded shoulder.

"The guy who's going to let you live," Bolan answered. He kept the pistol leveled at the man. "Tell Hamlin I'm going to be in touch. Soon."

"Right." The doorman sneered. "I know what you look like. You'd better be looking over your shoulder, because one day I'm going to be there, and my face will be the last thing you see."

Bolan figured the guy was putting on a show for the security camera in the corner of the room. He spoke quietly, his voice hard-edged. "Maybe you're right. I can always give Hamlin the message myself." He took aim with his weapon.

With a whimper, the doorman covered his face with his good arm.

Bolan dropped the pistol to his side and walked out the door.

The air outside was muggy, holding the threat of rain. People from the club were scat-

tered along the street in small groups, talking
and gesturing excitedly. Many of them fell silent when Bolan stepped into their midst. They
gave ground immediately.

Overhead, the windows of the club suddenly exploded, raining glass on the crowd.
Then the shrill keening of police and fire truck
sirens could be heard. The crowd quickly dis-
persed.

Bolan reached his car without being ob-
served. He started the engine and cut a U-turn,
heading back to the interstate. As he made the
corner, he saw the first police car screech to a
stop in front of the club. The cop got out and
spoke into a Handie-Talkie radio.

The Executioner turned the corner.

FIFTEEN MINUTES after he'd hit the after-hours
club, Bolan dialed Dennis Wynnewood's home
number. He knew from the police scanner under the car's dashboard that the media had arrived at the scene of the bombed club and were
shooting live tape.

"Hello," Wynnewood answered.

Even with caller ID, Bolan knew the lawyer
wouldn't be able to get the number of his cellular phone. Mobile transmissions tracked

back to relay stations, and would even shift as he left one field and entered another.

"We need to meet," Bolan said.

"I don't think so," Wynnewood replied.

Bolan could hear a television in the background that was tuned to an all-night news broadcast. "You saw what happened to the after-hours club."

"No." Abruptly the sound of the television disappeared.

"My next move is to come and see you," Bolan said, "if that's how you want to handle it."

"What do you want?"

"I want to know about that heart you brokered to Spencer Dane."

"There's nothing to know."

"You sold the heart." Silence strung out on the phone line and Bolan let it build, knowing it would get heavier on the lawyer.

"I don't have any names," Wynnewood said finally. "I just handled the cash."

"I want to talk to you about that."

"I can tell you about it over the phone."

"I don't think so."

"Look, I don't know where the heart came from. I didn't even know about Dane until they told me about him. I just followed up on what they gave me."

"Meet me at Metairie Cemetery," Bolan said. The cemetery was only minutes from his present position. He'd have time for a brief recon before the lawyer arrived.

"No," Wynnewood answered, but his voice lacked conviction.

"Be there at 5:45, Counselor," Bolan said firmly. "At the northeast corner." He punched the End button, then keyed in another number. A glance at his watch showed him Wynnewood had almost fifteen minutes to make the meet. That wouldn't give him enough time to arrange for protection with the police or his outside sources, but plenty of time to worry himself into a state where the deal Bolan offered him would look really good.

The phone was answered in the middle of the first ring. "Hamlin."

"Your boat, money and a business," Bolan said. "That's a pretty hefty tab so far, and I haven't been in town all that long."

"You son of a bitch. What do you want?"

"I want you to find out who's trafficking in stolen organs in New Orleans," the soldier told him. "Then I want you to tell me. You've got six hours to come up with something before I start costing you more money.''

''Why me?'' Hamlin demanded.

''Because when it comes to black-market profits around New Orleans, you're the guy with his finger in the most pies.''

''You know I'm not involved,'' Hamlin protested. ''Otherwise you'd be hunting me.''

''Somebody is,'' Bolan said. ''And you can put more muscle on the street than the cops. It's your choice if I stay interested in you.''

''You could have asked before you blew up my boat and my club.''

''I like to do business with a man who's properly motivated.'' Bolan found the off ramp leading to the cemetery. ''I'll be in touch, Hamlin.'' He punched the End button and cradled the phone.

The police scanner continued to churn out information about the after-hours club. As Bolan paused in the flow of traffic, he heard the dispatch officer contact a detective, letting her know a crime-scene unit was en route to a specified location.

The detective's code numbers were part of a set Bolan knew belonged to the Carrion Killings investigation. While he'd been out rattling cages, his targets clearly hadn't been idle.

DETECTIVE SERGEANT Marisa Ayshe saw the small cottage bathed in the lights from an emergency-rescue-unit vehicle and a marked NOPD patrol car. She also recognized Captain Lockspur's unmarked sedan.

She parked her Bronco behind the patrol car, grabbed her purse and got out. She wore cowboy boots, jeans, and a teal sweater over a black turtleneck against the early-morning chill. Her hair, which normally hung in small ringlets, was covered by a scarf. At thirty-six years of age, Ayshe's coffee-with-cream complexion remained unblemished and her figure still turned heads.

A policeman, wearing a rain slicker over his uniform and carrying his hat in one hand, stopped her at the entrance of the cottage. "I'm sorry, miss, but you can't go in there."

She took her shield from her purse and flipped it open.

"Sorry, Detective."

"No problem," she said. "Where's Lockspur?"

"In the house."

"What about the lady who made the call?"

"Mrs. Escudo? She's in the house too."

"Not her," Ayshe said. "Mrs. Desermeaux. Is she okay?"

"Yeah." The policeman grinned. "She's a tough old bird. She's already worked on the kid, and he was in pretty bad shape. She's some kind of doctor or something that these swamp people believe in. The captain doesn't hold with folk medicine and got kind of pissed off when he saw she'd been working on the kid. But I've seen a few things down in the parishes, and I know you can't just write that stuff off."

Ayshe thanked the man and went up onto the porch.

Lockspur was talking to a small man who held three little girls in his lap while he sat in a handmade rocker. The homicide captain was tall and broad, with a gunslinger mustache that grew thickly over a lip that was pulled slightly to the left by a scar that ran down his left cheekbone.

Ayshe knew from experience that Lockspur's stance indicated irritation. "Joe," she said softly as she entered the screened-in porch.

Lockspur turned. Without a word he walked over to her, grabbed her by the elbow and escorted her off the porch. "Are you out of your mind?" he demanded. "You're supposed to be undercover. If you get caught here by the press, we'll have lost a couple weeks' worth of work and a hell of a lead."

"My grandmother was the one who made the call." Ayshe extracted her elbow.

"The witch?"

"The *traiteur*."

A grin suddenly split Lockspur's face. In their five years of working together, Ayshe had seen the homicide captain smile only a handful of times. She'd never liked the effect. "That's your grandmother?"

"Yes. She left a message for me because she knew I was investigating the Carrion Killings."

Lockspur's face hardened again. "Have you talked to her about the investigations?"

"No. She'd heard about them through the grapevine. These swamp people know more than you give them credit for." Ayshe knew that was true because she'd grown up one of them. As a rookie, she'd worked some of the more primitive parishes before working her way into the New Orleans Police Department.

"Why are you here?" Lockspur asked.

"I wanted to make sure my grandmother was okay. She didn't talk directly to me. She left a message with Collins at the precinct. He didn't know how involved she was, and Dispatch wasn't exactly being informative."

"Your grandmother's just fine," Lockspur said, rubbing the back of his neck. "In fact, only a few minutes ago she was busy telling the ambulance people how to treat her patient."

Ayshe smiled at the image. "So what have you learned?"

After a brief hesitation, Lockspur reached into his pocket and flipped open a small notebook. "The boy's name is Tibob Escudo. He's eleven. His parents are Judithe and Didier. That's his father and three sisters on the porch. His mother's in the house with your granny."

"Is the boy going to make it?" Ayshe crossed her hands over her breasts, feeling suddenly cold. There'd been too many bodies over the past few weeks. A couple of them had been children.

"The medical team thinks so. He's been cut pretty good and had something removed, but the medical team doesn't know what, yet." Lockspur closed the notebook. "So far, that's all I've got. The father acts like he doesn't speak any English, and the mother's almost hysterical."

"He probably just doesn't trust you," Ayshe said.

"That's what I thought. I asked one of the deputies to scare up a local to act as an interpreter."

"Let me talk to him."

"Sure." Lockspur lifted his radio and addressed the uniforms, instructing them to seal off the area to the media. "Dispatch is handling this on the QT, but hell, the reporters can skim through the code stuff as well as we can."

Ayshe walked back onto the porch. When she spoke, it was in the French she'd learned at home. "Didier, do you know who I am?"

He glanced up at her.

"My name is Marisa Ayshe."

"The *traiteur*'s granddaughter. The one who's a police officer." He spit out the last word in English, obviously not impressed.

"That's right." Ayshe didn't let his resentment affect her. In her youth, she'd been on the other side. "We want to find out who did this to your son."

"It was a voodoo man," Escudo said. "He's made my Tibob into a zombie. He'll be a slave after he dies."

"He's not going to die. My grandmother has seen to that, and at the hospital he'll get well again."

Escudo shooed his girls off his lap and took a package of chewing tobacco from his overall pocket. He took a generous pinch, put it in his mouth and worked it into the side of his jaw. "What are you doing here?"

"We need to find the people responsible for hurting your son." Ayshe returned the man's challenging stare full measure. "He's not the first one they've hurt, and I don't think he's going to be the last. Not unless we stop them."

"I saw nothing."

"We're hoping Tibob did, so we'll need to talk to him. But we also need to look at everything we can."

Escudo looked at her. "Like what?"

"Who found him?"

"I did."

"Where?"

"Out in the bayou."

"Can you show us where?"

The man shrugged. Leaning forward, he spit out a stream of brown tobacco juice. "The bayous all look the same after a while. When I found Tibob I thought he was dead. The only thing I could think of was to bring him home to his momma."

Ayshe turned to Lockspur and switched to English, even though she felt certain Escudo could understand her. "He was probably out running illegal traps. He's reluctant to say where he found Tibob."

The homicide captain shifted his gaze to Escudo. "Tell him that I'm not a damned game ranger. I'm looking for the killers that almost murdered his son."

Ayshe translated, but Escudo still didn't seem convinced.

"It's dark in the swamps," he said. "You know that."

"Yes," she said, "but I also know that a hunter knows every inch of the land he hunts."

"Didier!" Judithe's voice cut in sharply. Her eyes were red from crying.

When she spoke, it was in English. "These people are here to help."

"Take them to where you found Tibob, or I will take them there myself."

For a moment, there was silence, then Escudo nodded. He glanced at Ayshe. "I will get my jacket."

Just then the medical crew emerged from the house bearing a stretcher. The boy aboard it looked pathetically small, and Ayshe's heart went out to him.

Marie Desermeaux followed them onto the porch. "*Grandmère,* are you well?" Ayshe asked worriedly. Only a few times over the years had she seen the woman appear so used up. The first time had been at the deathbed of Ayshe's father. Her mother had already run off to California with a man who'd promised to make her a movie star.

"I am fine, *cher,*" Desermeaux said. "It's just that these old bones are a little slower some mornings than others."

"What about the boy?"

"He will live. He has a strong heart. But he is one of yours, *cher,* one of them that the *bokor* has harmed."

"You're sure a voodoo man is behind this?" Ayshe had dismissed the possible voodoo link after the Rodriguiz woman's heart had turned up in Atlanta. But her grandmother's visions had never proved wrong before.

The old woman nodded. "Oh yes. I felt him when I attended the boy."

"Do you know who he is?"

Desermeaux shrugged. "Not yet, but when I see him, I will know him. Of this I am certain." She paused. "You must take care, too. I had a vision only a few moments ago. You will find this man who profits from the miseries of others. And when you do, you must hold on to life very tightly, or else you may lose it."

Ayshe shivered involuntarily. "How do you know the *bokor* profits from these people he harms?" Any mention of possible organ selling had been kept out of the media so far.

"I felt it."

Didier Escudo reappeared. He wore a cap that had seen better days and a lightweight jacket. He held a pair of hip waders in one hand and a 12-gauge shotgun in the other.

"What's with the gun?" Lockspur asked him.

"If I find these voodoo people, I will shoot their damn asses off."

"That might not be a bad idea," Ayshe muttered under her breath. Her own Glock 17 was in her purse.

"Can we get there by land?" she asked Didier.

He shook his head. "No. We go by joe boat." He started off for the shed that housed the vessel.

"Are you in or out?" Ayshe asked Lockspur.

"I'm in. Let me grab my jacket and a camera from my car."

"Marisa, you've been living the city life for a long time now, but don't forget what I've taught you," Desermeaux said.

"I won't," Ayshe promised. She hugged the old woman, then trailed after Escudo. She tried not to think of all the horror stories she'd been told as a small child. She hadn't really believed the tales then, but there were so many things she had seen in her career as a cop that she'd thought never existed. If child murderers could exist, then zombies didn't seem like that much of a stretch.

**3**

"I'm the guy you're waiting for," Bolan said as he stepped out of the gloom shrouding one of the elaborate tombs that dotted the graveyard. He had his hands beneath his duster, one fist gripping the butt of the .44 Magnum Desert Eagle.

Startled, Dennis Wynnewood jumped, then spun. He was a big man with glasses. He wore dress pants, an expensive pair of shoes and a long coat.

"Open your coat," Bolan ordered.

It took Wynnewood a moment to react. Then he held his coat open. A revolver was stuck in his waistband.

"Toss the gun away," the Executioner said.

"I just brought it in case," Wynnewood said. "These graveyards aren't exactly safe. People get mugged here during normal times, and Mardi Gras has never been anywhere near normal." Nevertheless he threw the gun ten feet away, where it came to rest at the base of a stone angel.

"Tell me about the heart," Bolan said.

Wynnewood looked uncomfortable. "I don't know the name of the guy who procured the organ."

"Then tell me what you do know."

The lawyer took a deep breath. "A few weeks ago, I got a note on my office e-mail. It had information about Spencer Dane and a phone number."

"You called it," Bolan stated.

"Yeah," Wynnewood nodded. "The money I was offered was too good to pass up. All I had to do was make a couple of phone calls to Dane's people and set things up. It didn't take them long to agree to the deal."

"What did you tell them?" Bolan asked.

Wynnewood shrugged. "Just what I was told to tell them—that a donor heart was coming available and did they want it. I didn't know about the Rodriguiz woman."

"But you do now."

"Yeah." Wynnewood slid his glasses up his nose. "I've been monitoring some things going on around the city. I've got some contacts at the police department.''

Bolan studied the man. ''This isn't the first time you've brokered organs.''

Wynnewood hesitated, obviously about to lie, then clearly thought better of it. ''No. That heart was the third one. I've handled one more since then.''

''What about the phone number you were given? Surely you checked it out.''

''You bet I did,'' Wynnewood retorted. ''When I logged on under the name I was given, a file was downloaded into my computer outlining the deal. An automatic deposit was also made into my bank account, ten percent up front. I got the other ninety percent when Dane's people paid off.

''Technically I'm not guilty of anything,'' Wynnewood went on. ''I didn't know anyone was being killed to get the organs. Not until the Rodriguiz woman. And I didn't find out about that until yesterday. Once I did find out, I knew I'd never be doing business with those people again.''

''If we were contesting that in a court of law, Counselor,'' the Executioner said, ''maybe a judge would listen to your argument. But I'm all the judge you're going to get right now, and it doesn't cut any ice with me. Tell me about this fourth deal you're involved with.''

"It's going down at four this afternoon," the lawyer said.

"Where?"

"At Chalmette National Historical Park. A woman's going to take possession of a kidney."

Bolan demanded the particulars. It was a good site, offering a number of escape routes. "Can you get in touch with these people?"

Wynnewood hesitated. "Maybe. They left me a contact name, but I haven't tried it. I've thought about looking up a list of people searching for organs and cutting deals myself, but I haven't. It's too damn chancy. So I just serve as the banker.''

"What did you do with the money when you got it?" Bolan asked.

"I deposited it in an account at an ATM in Jefferson Downs Racetrack in twenty-thousand-dollar increments.''

Bolan had to admit that was a smart thing to do. Using the ATM, with access to banking done with the race track as well, the deposits would be camouflaged. Money could be ferried from the track to any part of the city, and to other cities, with plenty of cutouts along the way.

"I'm ready to cut a deal," Wynnewood said.

Bolan fixed the lawyer with a hard stare. "What have you got to trade?"

"I can give you the names of the two other people I've done business with."

"That's something," Bolan conceded, "but not much. There's little incentive for them to roll over on the people they've been dealing with."

"I couldn't take prison."

Bolan let the thought hang heavily on the guy for a moment, then said, "Set up a deal."

"With what? These people want money up front."

"I've got it," the Executioner said.

Wynnewood looked nervous. "These people are dangerous. If I cross them, they're going to be looking for me. What kind of guarantee do I get that I'm going to be protected?"

"None," Bolan replied. "That's the deal, Counselor. Take it or leave it."

In the end, he took it.

"Let them know you're looking for another heart," Bolan said. "By the time you get to your office, you'll have a transmission waiting in your fax machine. Study it. When they ask you questions, make sure you know the answers."

"What about the money?" Wynnewood shifted self-consciously. "They'll ask."

Bolan took a package wrapped in brown paper—money he'd taken from Hamlin's yacht—from his coat pocket and handed it to Wynnewood. "There's fifty thousand dollars in here. Don't get the idea that you can take it and run. I'll come looking for you, and I'll leave you wherever I find you."

"How will I get in touch with you?" the lawyer asked.

"You won't," Bolan said. "I'll be in touch with you." Without another word, he turned and left, threading his way through the cemetery. He had no doubt that someone had gone into business for themselves in the city. Once he made a physical connection, he could start probing to see how big the operation was. Then he could work on taking it apart.

DEEP IN THE BAYOU, Arne Madigan watched the *bokor* with interest.

Papa Glapion was well into his fifties, a rotund little man with skin as black as coal, and a fringe of gray hair that ringed his otherwise bald head. He wore a shawl across his shoulders.

"You know me, don't you?" the *bokor* asked the woman, his voice taking on a singsong quality.

The woman struggled feebly against the two men who held her arms. Madigan guessed that she was in her late twenties. Naked from the waist up, perspiration gleamed on her skin.

Madigan could almost feel the fear radiating out of the woman as she continued to push against her captors. Madigan was a big man, topping out at six feet five inches and carrying two hundred fifty very solid pounds. His black hair was neatly cut, and he had a pale complexion. He wore a charcoal gray lightweight suit that he knew would be sticking to him by ten o'clock because of the humidity.

Madigan glanced at his two companions. Winston Chen wore a wide-brimmed hat with mosquito netting that dropped to his shoulders while his slim surgeon's hands were encased in a pair of gloves. In the past, he'd always enjoyed life's finer things, and it was only since being forced to leave Hong Kong that he'd had to make do with anything less than what he'd wanted.

"He's rather theatrical, isn't he?" Madigan said to his other companion.

"Personally," the woman replied, "I preferred the other ceremonies we've gotten to see. I rather liked watching them bite the heads off chickens."

Madigan studied Kaliope's face. He'd always found her particular blend of beauty and blood lust intoxicating. "Perhaps you can convince the good *bokor* to offer you a private showing later."

"Maybe I will," Kaliope replied.

The woman captive screamed as the two men tied her to stakes that had been pounded into the earth. When she was spread-eagled on the ground, still fighting her bindings, Papa Glapion grinned at Madigan.

"Now we begin. You will see my power."

Madigan watched with interest. The son of German immigrants, who'd settled in England, he'd learned early on that a man could get what he wanted with quick fists and a cunning brain. He'd gone to Hong Kong in the late seventies and soon established himself in the very lucrative area of trafficking in illegal goods between the British and the Chinese.

By the mideighties, he'd begun trafficking in human organs. It hadn't taken him long to put together a network that was gearing up to service a growing market. With transplantation techniques improving dramatically, he'd found his skills and talents much in demand. With the imminent return of Hong Kong to China, Madigan had decided to pull his operation to the United States.

Now, things were beginning to come together for him in America. The demand, filtered through a number of lawyers, corporations and other fronts, with finders fees being paid to employees within the United Network for Organ Sharing—UNOS—was increasing with Madigan's record of delivery. The heart they'd lost in Atlanta was the first time he hadn't come through.

Papa Glapion gestured, and a white-robed young woman came out of the shadows cast by torches that ringed the clearing, two candles in her hands. She did some kind of dance, then placed the candles on the ground. Three drummers began beating on their instruments, the tempo wild.

Madigan felt it throb into him and a kernel of fear lodged at the base of his spine. He shifted slightly, feeling the reassuring weight of the .451 Detonics Magnum Scoremaster against his side.

He saw that Kaliope was totally entranced by the proceedings. She'd been a terrorist in Greece when he'd met her. They hadn't become lovers—men as a general rule didn't hold much appeal for Kaliope. But her martial skills were tremendous. Over the years, she'd covered his back a number of times.

Papa Glapion picked up a clay jar and began a slow imitation of the dance the young woman with the candles had performed. He let a white powder from the jar trickle through his fingers, inscribing designs on the muddy ground. "This is the symbol of the *loa* we are invoking," he explained.

The *loa*, Madigan remembered from the earlier conversations with the *bokor,* were spirits—either good or evil.

The voodoo man then marked off the points of the compass with the powder. The torches around them kept burning, their flames reflected in the still bayou waters.

The young woman staked to the ground started to scream, but Madigan knew no one would hear her. They were too far from civilization.

Papa Glapion's followers joined him, and they began a slow dance.

"You know me," Papa Glapion said to the woman in a whisper that somehow carried over the hypnotic beat of the drums. "You know I have the power to make the dead walk."

Her screams continued, the muscles in her neck taut.

"I take your life now," Papa Glapion said, "and what I give back to you, I own." From his packet he took a small tube that looked like it had been carved from bone. He leaned close to his prisoner, put his lips to the tube and blew through it.

A fine, grayish white dust puffed out, coating the woman's face, settling into her open mouth, her eyes and her nostrils.

Around the woman, the dance continued. Her screams started to abate. Then one of the white-robed apostles handed the *bokor* a live dove. Papa Glapion took the bird and quickly snapped its neck.

He stood over the woman, then bit through the dead dove's neck, letting the blood pour over her face and upper body. Taking a small knife from his belt, he knelt and cut a line across her neck.

Madigan could tell that the blade hadn't gone deep enough to be lethal.

"I knew there had to be some bird biting in here somewhere," Kaliope said enthusiastically.

Madigan ignored her. The ceremony wasn't nearly as important as the end result. Outside the body, a liver lasted only six hours, a heart eight and the kidneys somewhere around four days. Taking prisoners was too chancy, and moving the organs around got tricky with the time constraints. One alternative had been to render the "donors" brain-dead and keep the bodies in storage, but heart-lung machines were expensive and noticeable. So far they'd been able to set up a base, complete with the most up-to-date medical facilities a surgeon could want. But there were still space limitations. The *bokor* offered a means of extending the viability of an organ.

Glapion lifted his hand to still the drums. He looked at Madigan. "She's dead."

"Impossible," Chen snorted. "You hardly broke the skin."

Papa Glapion stared down the Chinese doctor. "Come see for yourself."

Madigan led the way and stopped beside the woman. The *bokor* used his knife to sever the ties binding her to the stakes. She didn't move. Dropping into a crouch, Madigan stared into her glazed eyes. The gray-white powder had settled over them.

He reached forward, intending to pull her eyelid down. Papa Glapion seized his wrist.

"Don't," the *bokor* warned. "If you touch the powder now, with the spirits invoked, you, too, will become a zombie."

Madigan pulled his hand back.

"This magic," Papa Glapion said, "is not to be taken lightly."

"She is dead," Chen confirmed, "though I wouldn't have believed it if I hadn't seen it." He held her wrist in his fingers. "There's no pulse, no respiration." He pinched her flesh hard. "And no response to pain."

Papa Glapion laughed. "Of course she's dead. I killed her."

"Poison," Chen said. "Something definitely fast-acting." He spoke with a clipped

British accent, reflecting his background. "Bloody hell, I hope it won't infect more than the respiratory system. Maybe we can salvage her kidneys. Everything else, I'm sure we'll lose. There's no time to get her to the OR."

"I had a buyer for her heart," Madigan said. He fixed Glapion with a glare. "Dammit, man, if I'd known you were going to kill her right here, I'd have had a tech team ready to harvest her organs."

"You're forgetting that I have special powers," Glapion replied.

The *bokor* grabbed the woman's ankles and dragged her into the bayou. For a moment she floated, then Papa Glapion put a hand on her stomach and pressed her under the water.

He started praying loudly over her, using both hands to keep her submerged.

Perspiration was streaming down his face when he released the woman and spoke to her in bastardized French. Madigan understood enough to know the *bokor* was commanding the woman to get up.

"He's crazy," Chen said. "It's been six minutes since she was put under the water. She's dead. He's wasting his breath and our time."

The woman started flopping her arms, jerking like a puppet on a string. Then she stood upright, the muddy water streaming off her body.

Her features were blank, her skin lusterless. Her arms hung slackly by her side.

"See," Papa Glapion crowed. "She is not dead."

"It's impossible," Chen said.

"Neither is she alive," the *bokor* stated.

The hairs on the back of Madigan's neck started to rise.

Chen took a stethoscope from the black bag he'd brought with him. Placing the flat metal disk between the woman's breasts, he stuck the ends in his ears and listened intently. "I can't find a heartbeat," he told Madigan.

"That's because she's a zombie," Glapion said.

Madigan couldn't deny the proof standing before him.

"I FOUND HIM THERE." Didier Escudo pointed at the bayou bank and cut the boat's one-cylinder engine.

The flat-bottomed narrow craft was made of aluminum over a wooden frame, and it drifted easily in the slow current.

Under the canopy of cypress trees and Spanish moss, the night's shadows still lingered. Lockspur pointed his flashlight in the direction Escudo had indicated, flicking the beam through the tangle of trees.

Marisa Ayshe took up the small grappling anchor and tossed it expertly. When it caught in the lower branches of a tree on that side of the bank, she pulled the boat in.

Once she had the boat up on the bank, Ayshe slid her Glock from her purse and shoved it into the waistband of her pants. Her pulse quickened as she stepped onto the muddy ground. Switching on the flashlight her grandmother had given her, she took the lead. Lockspur followed her, cursing the underbrush that she seemed to avoid so easily. Escudo remained in the boat, his 12-gauge across his knees.

"How the hell do you walk through this without falling on your face?" Lockspur asked.

"Practice," Ayshe replied. "My father was a crawfisherman all his life. Whenever I wasn't in school, I helped him."

"I didn't know that."

"There's a lot you don't know about me," she said.

"I didn't know your grandmother was a witch," the homicide captain admitted. "That surprised me. How much do you know about that stuff?"

"Not even enough to sell a wart." Ayshe swept her flashlight around, then called to Escudo for directions. He waved them farther along.

"How do you sell a wart?" Lockspur asked.

"To get rid of a wart," Ayshe said, "you go to a *traiteur* like my grandmother. She'll rub the wart with a nickel, then tell you to spend it. Whoever receives your nickel will get your wart, too."

Ayshe's flashlight beam picked up a dark stain on the muddy ground to her right. She shone it over the patch.

A couple of water moccasins and a host of moths and beetles were feasting on the blood Tibob Escudo had left at the scene. Lockspur cleared his throat and swallowed noisily.

"If you're going to be sick," Ayshe warned him, "do it over there."

"I'm okay. It just caught me off guard."

"That's the swamp for you." Her own stomach felt queasy. "Anything that doesn't move fast enough or fight back hard enough gets eaten." She closed in with the flashlight, scaring the snakes away. The moths swarmed into the flashlight's beam.

"They couldn't have operated on the boy here," Lockspur said. He swatted at the moths that flew around him, then gave up and switched off his flashlight.

Ayshe turned off her own light. "They just dropped him here to die."

"Yeah." Lockspur focused his 35 mm camera and took some shots of the scene. "When we get the bastards who are behind this, they better go down for some serious time."

"They will," Ayshe promised.

"We need to get a crime scene unit in here." Lockspur put his camera away.

Ayshe nodded. "This tells us something already, though. These people, at least some of them, are familiar with the bayous."

"Yeah." Lockspur didn't look happy about the thought. "When you make that deal later today with Counselor Wynnewood, you might keep that in mind. These people might also be able to recognize you as a cop." He headed back to the boat.

For a moment, Ayshe lingered, looking at the blood on the ground. Despite the danger, she knew she couldn't back away from the upcoming assignment. The undercover team had made sure her ID was in place after they'd turned up the attorney who said he'd been approached by the organ-selling ring. He'd come forward quietly and offered his services.

She turned on her heel and followed Lockspur, her grandmother's warning ringing in her ears.

**4**

"I'm Special Agent Travis Fox of the FBI," Mack Bolan said, displaying his ID to Lockspur. The ID card was new—barely a half hour had passed since he'd picked it up at the courier service—but the case that held it was old and worn, as though it had been carried around for years.

They stood just outside the emergency room of Tulane Medical Center. Blue-uniformed nurses and orderlies ferried patients through the corridor with grim efficiency and bedside manners that had already worn thin.

"Have you ever been here when Mardi Gras was in full swing?" Lockspur asked, dodging a wheelchair.

"Yeah," Bolan said. But he'd never been there to enjoy the party atmosphere.

"The city becomes a zoo," Lockspur growled. It was only a little after eight o'clock.

After learning about the young boy the homicide team had brought into the hospital, Bolan had called the PD and found out that Lockspur was already on the scene. They'd arranged to meet at the hospital instead of the station.

From what he saw of the big homicide cop, Bolan liked the man. Lockspur was pulling hard duty in a hard city, and he was standing his ground.

"How's the boy doing?" Bolan asked.

"The last time I talked to the doctor," Lockspur said, "he didn't know if he was going to make it."

"I caught most of it over the scanner," the Executioner said. "Do you want to walk me through the rest of it?" As he listened, Bolan knew he wasn't getting everything. His combat radar told him that. Lockspur was holding something back.

"So, after I found the scene where they'd left the boy to die," Lockspur finished, "I got back to the hospital to see how he was doing."

"Is there any chance he'll recall what happened to him?"

Lockspur shrugged. "We don't know. There was an old woman out there, one of those bayou witch grannies you hear about, who told me she thought someone had tried to turn him into a zombie." He cocked an eyebrow. "Whacked-out, isn't it?"

Before Bolan could respond, a doctor in a stained smock stepped out into the hall and looked around.

"That's our man," Lockspur said, moving to intercept the doctor. When he caught up with him, he made the introductions. "Dr. Millford, this is Special Agent Travis Fox of the FBI."

The doctor's handshake was strong. "The boy seems to be out of any immediate danger," he said. "They cut out his pancreas, which did some damage to his liver. A surgeon almost always does when he starts mucking around with the pancreas. But the damage was kept to a minimum, which was surprising. From the way you said he was dumped, I got the impression they didn't much care whether he lived or died."

"I don't think they did," Lockspur said. "I think his survival was an accident."

"They didn't suture the boy up, but luckily the clamps held. Otherwise he would be dead. Still, he's lost an awful lot of blood." Millford cleared his throat. "He can survive without a pancreas. If he has the will to do so."

Bolan looked at the doctor. "What do you mean?"

Millford rubbed his forehead. "He was heavily sedated when he was brought in, but we couldn't identify the agent from the blood tests we ran. There were traces of a general anesthetic, but they were too old to account for the trance the boy appears to be in. I'm afraid there might have been some brain damage. Possibly some nerve damage, as well."

"Can we see him?" Lockspur asked.

Millford hesitated. "Briefly. He's going to be moved to the ICU as soon as we can clear a space for him." He led them back into the ER.

The boy seemed almost lost in the bed. His eyes were open, but he maintained a thousand-yard stare. A uniformed cop stood guard beside him.

A nurse came for Millford. He said a hurried goodbye and departed.

Bolan studied the ashen pallor of the boy and pushed himself past the anger he felt. "Where do zombies figure into this?"

Lockspur shook his head. "We don't know. We read it like you do—someone's set up a butcher shop in New Orleans and is selling organs to the highest bidder. It's happened before, but not to this extent."

"Any ideas who?"

"Nope. We checked with the United Network for Sharing Organs, but they also don't have any leads on this. There's big money in organs. Deals have been brokered where someone has sold one of their healthy kidneys to a dialysis patient. It's illegal as hell, but it's done."

Bolan stared into the boy's blank eyes. If it wasn't for the beeping machinery hooked up to him, he might have been dead.

"He's stabilized," a nurse said. She unhooked some of the equipment, then lifted the brakes on the bed's wheels. "If you'll excuse me, I've got to get him up to ICU. His mother's waiting to see him."

Bolan and Lockspur stepped out of the way.

"Let's get some air," the homicide captain said, "and we'll see about getting you up to speed." He led the way out of the ER and was met at the door by an attractive woman in street clothes.

Bolan caught the small head shake Lockspur gave her that warned her off. Already

committed to entering the ER, she passed Bolan, acting as if she was there to see someone
else.

The soldier had gotten a glimpse of her
mud-covered cowboy boots, the same mud
that Lockspur seemed to be sporting on his
shoes. The Executioner knew that Lockspur
was going to give him only part of the truth;
but that was all he was prepared to deal out, as
well.

"WE'RE HARVESTING the heart now," Arne
Madigan said, using the speakerphone func-
tion. He paced the floor of the office, pausing
at the half wall of glass that looked down into
the operating room. "Do we have the liver sold
or not?"

"Thomsen's dragging his feet about it." The
voice belonged to a Dallas attorney who'd
once done a lot of work for the oil tycoons in
Texas. She'd been cut from a fat retainer when
the oil boom hit bottom, but had maintained
her contacts for occasional work. Madigan's
recruiting network had turned her up. Angie
Dawson was hungry enough to go hunting
through the oil-rich barons who found out
wealth couldn't protect them from diseased or
used-up organs.

"Why?"

"The price."

"It's not going to change," Madigan said.

"He says he's also not sure about the tissue matches. He's scared the liver won't take."

Madigan stared through the glass. In the operating room, Chen and his team were getting down to it. The room was huge and had originally held oil-refinement equipment, pumps and storage containers.

Scalpel in hand, Chen made the first incision across the woman's exposed torso, unzipping her flesh from neck to pubis. Then he began cutting through the sternum with a surgical saw, its high-pitched whine swallowed by the soundproofed walls. A drain had been placed in the center of the OR so everything could be hosed down for rapid cleaning. Chen and his crew had already worked two other "donors" since the foray into the swamp. The bodies had been taken back into New Orleans to be dumped. Madigan didn't want anything left around that could lead back to their headquarters.

"Thomsen's doctors looked at the tissue samples we sent them," Madigan said. "They know we have as good a match as we can under the circumstances. I've got a prospective list for this goddamned liver as long as my arm. You give him a call and tell him this is his last chance. I'm ready to move on to the next guy in line.'' He ended the call, then punched in another number and lined up the secondary unit in Tulsa, Oklahoma. If Thomsen didn't close the deal, there was the lady in Tulsa who'd been able to come up with thirty thousand dollars less but who was ready to go through with it immediately.

He took out the remote control for the twenty-seven-inch television that sat on the right-hand side of the room. When he switched it on, the image was relayed from the camera mounted inside the OR. He adjusted the volume. Chen's voice came through clearly as he called out orders to his staff.

The rest of the office held the usual office equipment, Spartan apart from two luxurious items, a Persian floor rug he'd splurged on and a baby grand piano that stood in the center of the room.

The office door opened and Kaliope walked in. She had a room on-site too, but Madigan had never been inside it. She maintained her distance from everyone, and he'd learned to honor it.

"I see you're watching Chen operate," she said, seating herself on the edge of the desk.

"Yes."

"He's not using an anesthetic," Kaliope said.

Madigan used the remote control to zoom in on the woman's face. No oxygen mask covered her nose and mouth, but she didn't move.

"It'll be interesting," Kaliope said, "to see if Glapion's mumbo jumbo is still going to work after they take her heart out."

Returning the camera's focus to its original setting, Madigan relaxed back in his chair.

Kaliope looked at him, her odd-colored eyes managing to look both seductive and innocent. "I've heard that zombies move."

Madigan laughed. "Only on late-night movies."

"Care to make a little wager on it?" she asked. "I've never seen a zombie before this morning. Seeing her come up out of that water like that tends to make a believer out of one."

"It didn't work on the boy," Madigan pointed out. "He fought until we sedated him.

Glapion's zombie dust didn't have much of an effect on him.''

"Maybe not everyone's susceptible."

"Okay, a thousand bucks," he said.

"Done."

They turned back to watch the operation.

Madigan's fax machine spit out a sheet of paper. He picked up the paper and scanned it briefly. "It's from Dennis Wynnewood. He says he needs a heart now, as well, and has fifty thousand dollars up front for it."

Kaliope eyed him speculatively. "He didn't do too well with the last heart deal he brokered in Atlanta."

"Yes." Madigan considered the fax again. "I like money, but not when there's a lot of risk attached to it."

"If we work it right, we can take the money and leave Wynnewood in no position to tell anyone anything," Kaliope suggested.

Madigan thought for a moment, then nodded. "I agree." He glanced at his watch. "The other deal we made with him is supposed to take place at four this afternoon at that park."

"Right."

"Then let's meet him earlier and take the money off his hands."

The phone rang. The lines were scrambled through a satellite receiver ten miles away, then relayed to the site. Madigan picked it up.

"Thomsen wants the liver," Dawson said.

"Fine. And the money?"

"It's already been transferred to your account."

Madigan keyed up the computer and checked. The money was in the bank. "The organ's on its way." He broke the connection, then initiated the computerized program that would transfer the money into the accounts he maintained under a cover in the Caribbean.

That done, Madigan watched Chen pack the heart and liver in the waiting ice coolers, then turn off the heart-lung machine.

Without warning, the woman on the operating table lurched up, knocking over the tray of surgical instruments. Blood gushed from the incisions crossing her body.

"Jesus bleeding Christ," Madigan said, leaning into the television screen.

The woman reached out with her arms, then fell back and lay still.

"Chen," Madigan yelled through the intercom that connected him to the OR. "What the hell was that?"

The surgeon was visibly shaken. "Nerve reflex," he said. "It wasn't until we turned off the heart-lung machine that her brain told her she was dying."

"Get that mess cleaned up." Madigan switched off the intercom. He didn't think he'd be watching many more of the harvesting operations in the future.

He walked over to the wet bar set up in the corner and poured himself a double Scotch whiskey, neat, and drank it down without pause. He shivered. "Jesus." He looked at Kaliope, who seemed more intrigued by the gruesome display than appalled.

She held out her hand. "You owe me a thousand dollars. The zombie moved."

THERE WAS NOTHING NEW in the information the NOPD's homicide division had regarding the Carrion Killings. Mack Bolan finished going through the files Captain Lockspur had passed on to him since leaving the Tulane Medical Center.

They were at a small diner, and Lockspur was at the back using the pay phone. When he saw that Bolan was finished with the materials, he ended his conversation and crossed the dining area.

"There's not a whole lot, is there?" Lockspur asked, sliding back into the booth.

"No. Maybe you want to tell me what you've got working."

Lockspur leaned against the padded seat. "After I got your call this morning, I started thinking. I figured that if Senator Harris Mercury really pulled some weight in Washington, I should have had a bunch of FBI guys crawling around with microscopes about now. Instead, I got you." He held up his forefinger. "One guy."

He began toying with his walkie-talkie, which he'd placed on the table. "At first I thought maybe the Bureau was just paying lip service to Mercury's demands for justice over what had happened to his stepson. But you don't act like a cop. You don't ask enough questions, and you don't make the usual moves."

"Maybe you should check me out."

"I already have. It was the first thing I did. But the two guys I talked to didn't seem to know much more about you than what I'd read in the jacket I pulled."

"I've been undercover," Bolan said. "I worked the Boston Mafia in deep for a few years."

"That," Lockspur stated, "I believe. You're a gamer. You like going it alone. Otherwise you'd have backup here. That's one of the cardinal rules the feebs seem to go by. But that doesn't seem to be the way you work."

"I'm here in an observational capacity," the Executioner reminded him. "If it turns out more help is needed down here, I'll get it. Believe that."

Lockspur nodded. "I do. But I also believe that you're not really a cop. You're like a sniper waiting for a target to pop up."

Pulling a report from his briefcase, Bolan said, "If you're through playing *What's My Line,* I'd like to talk to you about something else."

Lockspur looked at the manila file folder Bolan laid on the table. "What's that?"

"The Escudo boy's medical file."

"How'd you get that? I haven't even got my copy yet. It's not supposed to be ready until later on."

Bolan didn't reply. Kurtzman had broken into the medical center's computer files and pulled it after Bolan had contacted him.

After a strained moment, Lockspur said, "Okay, what have you got?"

"Not all of the blood on the Escudo boy was his own."

"Dr. Millford didn't say anything about that." Lockspur turned the file around and began to scan it. "And the lab boys searched the crime scene, but not the kid because the EMT people already had him. We've still got his clothes. We should be able to check those."

"One of the nurses at the hospital typed the blood," Bolan replied. "Millford still may not know."

"It says here that the blood wasn't human, that it probably belonged to some kind of bird."

"Yeah. They sacrifice birds in voodoo ceremonies, don't they?" Bolan asked casually.

"Sometimes. Most of the nonauthentic ones just pour a lot of alcohol around and do a little fire-eating. It makes the tourists happy, though."

"Do you know anyone in the voodoo circles in the city who could be tied up with the organ-brokering ring we're looking for?'' Bolan asked.

"If I did, then I'd be able to find the people out there stealing organs,'' Lockspur responded sharply.

"You've got files on the voodoo circles.''

Lockspur shrugged. "Vice does. Anybody who does voodoo and kills somebody during the course of it, we lock them away. But vice will know who the con artists and hucksters are.''

"It might be worth checking through those files,'' Bolan said. "Somebody who usually works small may have decided to hit the big time.''

Lockspur's agreement was grudging. "I'll pull a couple of uniforms and have them do the prelim search.''

Abruptly the walkie-talkie squawked into life. "Ocean Thirteen, this is Dispatch.''

Lockspur squelched the volume and keyed the mike. "Ocean Thirteen reads you, Dispatch. Go ahead.''

"Roger, Ocean Thirteen, I've got a patch-through for you.''

"Put it through.''

"Ocean Thirteen," a man's voice said, then gave his badge number. "I'm down in the French Quarter working mounted patrol. A few minutes ago, the manager of the Lafayette Royale motel called me about a couple of suspicious-looking people who'd checked into the motel. Me, I'm wondering how the hell she can spot anybody acting suspicious in the middle of Mardi Gras, but I go check it out anyway. She described their van to me, and I found it out in the parking lot. There was blood in the back of it. I started thinking of the Carrion Killings because you people said they might be using vans to work out of."

Lockspur was already shoving his way out of the booth. "Stay there," he told the officer. "Don't touch anything, but don't let them leave. And for Christ's sake, get that tag number.

"Come on," Lockspur said, climbing into the unmarked car out in the parking lot. "We'll take mine."

Bolan slid into the passenger seat and belted himself in as Lockspur keyed the ignition, backed them out of the parking lot in a screeching U-turn, then roared into the flow of traffic amid angry honks.

Lockspur handed Bolan a whirling cherry, and he set it on the dashboard so it could be seen through the windshield. Then he loosened the Desert Eagle inside its shoulder leather. If they caught the organ-brokering ring disposing of corpses, the warrior knew they wouldn't go down easy.

**5**

The Lafayette Royale motel contained about thirty two-storied units, the architecture a mix of Creole and Deep South. Half-moon balconies held flowering bougainvillea that wound through the wrought-iron railings and along the sloping roof.

Bolan could hear sounds of Mardi Gras revelry coming from a block away as Lockspur pulled into the parking lot near the patio behind the motel. A five-foot-high brick wall with iron spikes mounted on top surrounded the property.

Twenty-four-year-old Officer Gerald Downs stood half-hidden beside his mount near an arched gate leading into an alley. He pointed out an old Dodge van in the parking area, and passed on the room number the people had been given.

"Ocean Thirteen," Lockspur's radio squawked. "I've got the ID on that van that was called in."

"Go ahead," Lockspur said, gazing up at the motel.

"The vehicle is registered to a David Hightower. His mother reported him missing after he hadn't been home for three days."

"Roger, Dispatch," the homicide captain said. "How's the backup coming?"

"Two uniformed units are on their way, and X-ray Nine is also en route. They should be there in about fifteen minutes. Two more mounted uniforms are also on their way."

Lockspur acknowledged the information and hung up the handset. He glanced at Bolan. "Fifteen minutes is too long, especially if there's a chance that this David Hightower is still alive."

"I agree," Bolan said. "Let's go." He opened the door and stepped out, leaving his jacket open.

They crossed the parking area and darted across the patio, where a few guests sat under umbrellas around a fountain.

"Number 22's at the end," Bolan stated.

"Got it," Lockspur said. He held a Colt .45 Government Model in his fist.

"I'm going in high," Bolan told him.

"Fine, I've got your back."

With his combat senses on full alert, Bolan stopped beside the door of number 22 and waited a heartbeat while the homicide captain fell into place on the other side.

They could hear voices coming from within. Then they smelled gas.

"Ready?" Bolan asked.

Lockspur nodded.

Gripping the Desert Eagle in both hands, the Executioner kicked the door open and whirled into the entrance. He swept the room from right to left.

A small living room led into a kitchenette, where a figure dressed in a clown's costume was opening the petcocks on the gas range. The clown brought up an Uzi machine pistol and fired it in a long, ripping burst of 9 mm parabellum rounds that chewed into the living room walls.

Bolan fired twice, hitting the clown in the chest. The heavy 240-grain boattail bullets drove the clown backward, blood splotching his costume.

Already in motion, the Executioner turned his attention to the stairway on his left. Another clown figure stood halfway down the steps, a sawed-off shotgun in his hands.

"Get down!" he yelled to Lockspur. The homicide detective wheeled back out of the doorway. Bolan went to ground only a moment before a double-aught pattern ripped up a section of the carpet where he'd been standing and ricocheted through one of the big paned windows. He fired the Desert Eagle three times, starting at the clown's knees and following the hand cannon's natural rise.

The bullets hit the man in the thigh, abdomen and collarbone. Spun by the force, the clown tumbled down the stairs, coming to rest in a heap at the bottom.

Bolan moved forward, holding the Desert Eagle on the man, and kicked the shotgun away from him. Blood leaked from the corner of the clown's mouth, staining the white greasepaint that covered his face.

Lockspur took a pair of cuffs from the back of his belt and fastened one end around the clown's wrist and the other to the stair railing.

The Executioner reloaded the big .44, then charged up the stairs with the pistol held before him. Two rooms were at the top of the steps. Glancing through the open door of one, he saw that it looked out over the alley. It was also empty.

The smell of gasoline was coming from the other room. Then there was the sound of something exploding, followed by the shattering of glass.

He tried the door but it was locked. He set himself to kick it open just as the first wisps of smoke curled out from under the door. The door still held after his first kick, but the jamb started to splinter.

Bolan kicked again and the door flew open. He charged into the room, taking in the broken window overlooking the patio.

"Call the uniform," Bolan told Lockspur, who'd come up behind him. "They're going to try to get away in that direction."

Lockspur spoke urgently into his walkie-talkie, then snatched the fire extinguisher mounted on the wall in the hallway.

Two bodies, a white male and a brown-skinned female, lay naked on the bed. Their abdominal wounds showed that they were beyond help and had probably been dead for hours.

"Dammit," Lockspur swore when he saw the corpses. He used the fire extinguisher to beat back the flames.

Bolan looked out the window. Two fleeing clowns raced across the courtyard, shoving people out of their way and overturning tables. An umbrella floated upside down in the fountain.

Officer Downs had stepped out in front of them with his gun drawn. His voice carried across the courtyard. "Police! Drop your weapons!" His stance was textbook perfect.

The clowns didn't break stride as they fired. Downs crumpled.

Bolan braced his arm against the window-frame and lifted the Desert Eagle. He shut out the heat of the flames and concentrated on the targets before him. The distance was seventy yards. Coupled with the downward angle at which he had to shoot, he was pushing the envelope for accuracy. His finger tightened on the trigger, taking up the slack.

A double-cab orange pickup suddenly roared through the main entrance to the parking area, heading straight for the running clowns. The truck's driver brought the vehicle around in a sideways skid that smashed it up against a parked subcompact. The clowns didn't hesitate about making for the truck.

Bolan fired two shots at his first target. The clown fell to the ground, landing on his face.

The survivor redoubled his efforts to reach the getaway vehicle, hunkering down to provide a smaller target. An assault rifle cut loose from the passenger side of the pickup, shattering the tiles that formed part of the roof overhang under the window.

Bolan fired three more times, a rolling burst of thunder that swept over the other clown and knocked him down. He fired the last three shots at the pickup, punching holes in the door and windshield.

With its rear wheels whining as the driver threw it into gear, the pickup smashed into another parked car, then rode roughly over it.

The Executioner changed magazines, then threw himself through the broken window. Autofire raked the roof and the front of the motel. The warrior stayed low, sliding like a base runner stealing third. The rough shingles tore at his pant leg. The pickup straightened out as Bolan reached the end of the roof and launched himself outward.

He came down on his feet, going immediately into a roll to absorb the shock of hitting the ground. Bullets rent the air and smacked into a soft drink machine on the sidewalk behind him.

Pushing himself up, he sprinted toward the fallen police officer. The pickup roared toward the entrance fronting the street.

Downs had been hit in the leg and in his side, but he seemed to be holding his own. "I'm okay," he said, taking a fresh grip on his revolver.

"Hang on," Bolan said. "Help's on the way." He shed his suit jacket as he ran toward the horse Downs had tethered to the gate. He untied the reins, then put his foot in the stirrup. The horse reared, its eyes rolling white.

Grabbing the pommel, the soldier vaulted into the saddle and fisted the reins, taking charge of the animal. He kicked his heels into the animal's flanks and urged it forward.

The orange pickup was just clearing the corner at the other end of the alley ahead of them. Bolan kicked the horse again and it responded with everything it had, its hooves ringing against the pavement.

They came left around the corner, narrowly avoiding a hot dog vendor and sending the people standing in line scattering. Bolan reined in the horse and kept to the sidewalk. He stayed low, riding along the horse's neck, and guiding the animal as much with his body as with the reins. They began to gain on the pickup, cutting its lead to twenty yards.

Enough cars were parked along the curb so that the team in the pickup didn't see Bolan at first. It was in the opposite lane, and the driver was concentrating on the traffic in front of him.

At the end of the block, the pickup slowed, getting ready to make a left turn.

Bolan brought the animal broadside to the pickup, raised his Desert Eagle and fired. The .44 round hit the windshield on the driver's side, and myriad tiny cubes of glass blossomed across its surface. He knew he'd missed the driver by inches. The guy on the passenger side leaned out, holding a CAR-15 rifle in one hand. As the gunner squeezed the trigger, the driver stepped on the accelerator. The ragged line of autofire didn't come close to the Executioner or his mount, but zigzagged up the side of the shop behind him and ripped through a street lamp hanging overhead.

The horse reared as the pickup screamed toward it. Bolan held the animal in check just long enough to get off his next round. When the Desert Eagle jumped against his palm, he kicked the horse's sides. The animal veered away from the pickup with a foot to spare.

Wheeling the horse, Bolan watched the pickup go out of control and smash into a low, stone wall on the other side of the street. It came to a jarring stop with the passenger side facing the warrior.

Two men with assault rifles clambered out the doors, bringing up their weapons.

With six bullets left in the big .44, the Executioner let loose with three rounds at each man. Neither gunner got off more than half a magazine. The 5.56 mm tumblers smashed the front windows of another store and took out a corner streetlight. The Desert Eagle's 240-grain bullets hammered the men into the side of the pickup, and they slid lifelessly to the ground.

Bolan ejected the spent clip, rammed a fresh one into the Desert Eagle and urged the horse into motion again, working around to the driver's side.

The driver was dead, slumped over the steering wheel with the back of his head missing. But the guy who'd been riding behind him wasn't there.

"Hey!"

Bolan turned the horse toward the sound of the voice.

An old man with a shock of white hair stood in front of a bakery. "That fella ran that way, mister," he said, pointing out the direction.

The Executioner found his quarry up ahead, shoving his way through the crowd on the sidewalk.

Bolan nudged the horse and the animal lunged forward, closing the sixty-yard gap easily.

The gunner moved out into the stalled line of traffic and tried to yank open a car door, but it didn't yield. He raised his pistol and pointed it at the driver.

Unable to get off a clear shot at the man, Bolan fired a round into the air.

The gunner's head jerked around. He fired twice but missed both horse and rider.

The gunner had reached the end of the street. He wheeled, unable to run any farther, and brought up his pistol.

The horse thundered down on him. Bolan felt the impact slam through the animal's frame before they regained their balance.

The man lay on the curb, gasping for breath, his eyes closed. His gun had landed almost ten feet away.

Bolan swung out of the saddle. He searched the kitbag belted across the front of the saddle and found a pair of handcuffs. Leaving the sweating horse ground tethered, he walked over to his prisoner.

The man looked up at him. "I think my leg's broken," he said.

"Over on your face," Bolan ordered. He felt little compassion for the man when he remembered the two bodies that had been left at the motel to be burned.

The man rolled over with a groan.

Bolan slipped the cuffs on him while a crowd started to gather.

"You got the boy, eh?"

Bolan looked up and saw the white-haired old man. "Yeah. Thanks."

"Well, he sure be a fast one, that boy." He rubbed his chin and chuckled. "If he was running a regular footrace, I'd sure be tempted to bet on him." He looked at Bolan. "He told you he gonna put the hex on you yet?"

Bolan shook his head. Down the block, he could see Lockspur's car trying to make its way through the traffic.

"Well," the old man said, "he might. That fella be a voodoo man, sure enough."

"What makes you say that?" Bolan asked.

The old man pointed to the necklace hanging out of the man's shirt. A gold chain held a small bag made out of red flannel. "That be a charm, I bet you."

Bolan knelt and pulled the bag from the necklace. He opened it and emptied the contents into his hand. A number of small bones lay in his palm.

"That be a gris-gris," the old man said. "Probably bones from some snake that was hoodooed into a good-luck charm for this guy."

"If you touch those bones, you are going to die," the gunner said. His face was tight with pain. "That was a powerful charm."

"It didn't seem to do you much good today." Bolan scattered the bones on the curb next to the man. "Who're you working for?"

His captive gave him a cold look. "I want a lawyer. I'm not saying anything."

The old man laughed and shook his head. "Them be magic words too. This voodoo man doesn't depend on just charms and such."

Lockspur made his way through the crowd, flashing his badge. "Is he still alive?"

Bolan nodded.

"Good," the homicide detective said as he reached for the handcuffed prisoner. "I'd need a seance to be able to question those other guys from the pickup."

Holding the flannel bag in his hand and trying to fathom the meaning of the ink markings that covered it, Bolan said, "This would be the town for it."

AN HOUR AND A HALF later, Bolan was cruising in the Stealth. Back at police headquarters, Lockspur had parked him in an office in the homicide division. Bolan had stayed there for an hour, waiting to see if the captain would give him anything to work with. The only real accomplishment he'd made was a change of clothes and a phone call to an FBI bureau chief who was in on the cover. The upshot was that Special Agent Travis Fox was still actively on the case, something that didn't sit well with

Lockspur, who'd hoped Fox would be pulled back.

Bolan had also hung on to the flannel gris-gris bag and gotten pictures of the people who'd been disposing of the bodies.

The Executioner had his other lines of contact apart from the homicide department. He dialed Dennis Wynnewood's office number on the car phone and used the cover name they'd agreed on to get him past the lawyer's secretary.

"Wynnewood." He sounded anxious.

"Did you make contact?" Bolan asked.

"Yeah," Wynnewood said. "Look, are you sure you want to do this? I don't know anything about these people except that they're willing to rip organs out of anybody they can. I don't know if they trust me. And there's an FBI guy in town who's putting the heat under the homicide division over the Carrion Killings. Maybe now's not the best time."

"Did you set up a meeting with them?" the Executioner went on, ignoring the lawyer's comment.

Wynnewood sighed. "Yes."

"When and where?"

"At noon. At the Bayou Bar Restaurant."
Wynnewood gave Bolan its location.

The soldier knew the area. "Make sure
you're there."

"Where are you going to be?"

"I'll be around," Bolan said.

"Do you want me to give them the money?"

"Yes. And don't be late."

Bolan punched the End button on the
phone, then called the Stony Man Farm cut-
out number. Brognola came on the line at the
other end.

"You are straining the relationship between
the New Orleans Police Department and the
FBI," the head Fed said.

Bolan allowed himself a small smile. "That
goes two ways. Lockspur is dedicating himself
to freezing me out of the play. So I'm keeping
the NOPD only as an option. Other things are
starting to break loose." He quickly brought
the Stony Man liaison up-to-date on the
Wynnewood development.

"Do you think they're going to bite?"
Brognola asked.

"Yes." Bolan wheeled through the traffic.
In the rearview mirror he could see a flatbed

trailer with a parade float atop it join the procession toward the French Quarter.

"They may take a whack at Wynnewood," the big Fed pointed out.

"I can cover Wynnewood long enough to get him out of the line of fire."

"He might try to turn state's evidence. Do we sit on him, or let him go to the police?" Brognola asked.

Bolan had already thought that scenario through. "Let the NOPD have him. If Wynnewood tells them what he knows, they might be more willing to step up their investigations."

"They're going to be pretty angry when they find out that Special Agent Fox had access to him but didn't give him up."

"True, but there's not a hell of a lot they can do about it. They're playing their own investigation close to the vest." Bolan stopped at a traffic light. A crowd of costumed revelers crossed the street, waving gaily at the stalled traffic.

"The operation here is big, Hal," Bolan said. "I've pushed everywhere I could get a handhold, and so far I'm not coming up with much for all the effort. From the case files

Lockspur showed me, there are forty-one possible victims.''

"Christ," Brognola said. "That's six more than the FBI figured, and two more than we had." '

"There's a lot of political pressure on the situation," Bolan replied. "I think the media down here know more than they're letting on, but they're keeping quiet."

"Because they don't want to scare anyone away?"

"Right. And these are professionals we're dealing with. Forty-one victims, fifty-seven transactions for organs and they've only dropped the ball once in the last three months."

"Hell, the fact that we didn't even tumble to them until recently says a lot, too."

"What about the pictures I faxed?" Bolan asked, referring to the pictures of the killer clowns and the backup group from the motel he'd sent.

"Kurtzman tagged them. When we've finished talking, I'll send it back your way. There's not much there, though. All of them had records in burglary, armed robbery, or loan sharking. But they were strictly small-time operators.''

"Any affiliations that I can work on?''

"Nothing definite. These guys have been around the block. If you find a brand on them, it'll be new.''

"I was thinking we might start looking into the other end of this operation,'' Bolan said.

"Which end?''

"Transportation. These people harvest the organs somewhere around New Orleans, so they've only got a hours'-long radius they can transport before transplantation has to begin.''

"Any ideas?''

"They have to be working the transports out of the airports,'' Bolan said. "We learned that from what went on in Atlanta. Maybe some of the local hops to Texas or other surrounding states could be accomplished by a puddle jumper, but to make it to Atlanta, they have to have access to jets, too.''

"Perhaps they use a charter service,'' Brognola suggested.

"Yeah. It might make sense to find out if any new services have started up lately, or if any old ones have changed owners.''

"I'll get the Bear to put someone on it. Let me know if there's anything else I can do."

"Sure." Bolan cradled the phone. An instant later the fax machine spit out the jackets Kurtzman had turned up on the gunners. Bolan leafed through them while he made his way through the slow grind of traffic. Brognola was right: there wasn't much. He fingered the red flannel bag that had contained the grisgris. He had another angle to hedge his bets on.

"THERE'S BEEN A PROBLEM with the Dreyser acquisition," Kaliope said.

"What?" Arne Madigan turned from the railing of the offshore drilling rig.

"The pickup team missed him. For a week he's been Mr. Reliability. Once we knew his schedule, we had him. Until a few minutes ago."

"They lost him?"

The woman nodded, the wind blowing across the drilling rig ruffling her hair. "There was no reason to think he would deviate from his schedule. The team held back a little too far and lost him in the traffic. They didn't sweat it because they knew he was headed to his dentist's office, but he never made it. I had our computer people break into his dentist's files, and they found out there was no appointment.''

"Dreyser lied."

"Yes."

Madigan turned over what he remembered about the man. Dreyser was a state auditor working in New Orleans—a stable, reliable man. The only thing special about him was the fact that his blood type was AB negative, and his tissue samples closely matched those of an aging shipping lines magnate in Chicago. The magnate was at this moment in a private clinic. The transplant team was expecting delivery within the next couple of hours.

Madigan looked out over the waters of the Gulf of Mexico. Dreyser's heart represented millions of dollars in profit, one of the best scores of the month. The shipping magnate also knew others who would be interested in Madigan's wares, and was willing to provide a list of potential clients—provided his operation was a success, of course.

The drilling rig on which Madigan stood was a legitimate operation—on the books, anyway. Madigan had searched for a dependable base of operations to open up his American business enterprises. The offshore drilling rig in the Gulf of Mexico provided him with easy access to most of the South.

He'd leased the jack-up barge from a wild-cat drilling operation that had been hitting nothing but dry holes for too long to stay competitively solvent.

Madigan had hired a pirate drilling crew whose members knew how to keep their mouths shut about anything strange that happened aboard the oil rig. They also didn't mind killing anyone who needed killing.

The organ dealer had every intention of extending his operation as far as he could. New Orleans was only a test run, a means of getting the bugs out of the system and setting up the necessary contacts. Dreyser's heart was an essential part of the plan.

"Tell them to go back over Dreyser's credit records that indicate where he might have been during some of his other dental appointments," Madigan said.

Kaliope nodded and spoke into the cellular phone she held.

Madigan checked his watch. They would be pushing it to make the meeting with Dennis Wynnewood. He'd started down the metal stairs leading to the helicopter pad at the base of the rig when Kaliope caught up with him.

"There's something else," she said.

He looked at her.

"The team that disposed of the two bodies this morning was caught by the police. Only one of them survived."

"Does he know anything?"

"Probably not. He was one of Glapion's people."

Madigan had put the *bokor* on retainer and assigned disposal of some of the corpses to him. All of the dead were flown back to New Orleans to ensure that the investigation remained concentrated in the city. Also, Madigan had access to some of the police personnel, and he could keep tabs on the investigation. "How did it happen?"

"A policeman called it in before Glapion's people were able to torch the motel room. Lockspur got there with an FBI agent named Travis Fox. It was Fox who killed those seven men and captured the remaining one."

"He's quite a worker," Madigan said dryly.

"Yes."

He swung up into the copilot's seat of the waiting helicopter. "Put someone on him, as well. He seems to be someone we'll need to take care of.''

Kaliope took up one of the rear seats. ''Maybe I should attend to him myself.''

Madigan looked at her as the helicopter took off, recognizing the blood lust in her mismatched eyes. ''If it comes to that,'' he said, ''do it.''

## 6

The white-haired old man's name was LaSalle Del Sesto, and he didn't work at the bakery, he owned it. When Bolan went into the bakery, Del Sesto remembered him at once and waved away Bolan's FBI ID. After the soldier explained his quest, the man offered to take him to Madame Calista. "She knows some voodoo," Del Sesto said. "She also knows some of the Tarot reading, seances and gives ghost tours in the Quarter to all the haunted houses. I think she can tell you who made that bag."

After a brisk ten-minute walk, they climbed a flight of narrow stairs to Madame Calista's second-floor office.

At the top of the stairs, Del Sesto rapped sharply on the frosted pane of glass. Faded gold lettering advertised Madame Calista, Mistress of Things Occult and Supernatural.

"Please enter," a woman's whiskey baritone called out.

"That's her working voice," Del Sesto said, turning the door handle.

Bolan followed the man into a small office. A musty smell pervaded the room, and the windows were covered by black muslin, blocking out all natural light. Wall shelves contained pots and jars, books and various other artifacts. On an ancient wooden desk, a stuffed raven perched on a human skull. A fountain pen lay next to an inkwell, a pad of paper with a border of zodiac signs beside it.

The woman in the swivel chair behind the desk was easily twenty years too old for the long, flowing black wig she wore. Worked silver earrings dangled to her shoulders. Her high-collared black dress concealed some of her weight.

"This here's an FBI agent, Del Sesto said, introducing Bolan. He shot them boys this morning."

Bolan placed the gris-gris on the desk, following it with a fifty-dollar bill. "LaSalle told me he thought you might be able to identify where this came from."

Calista reached into a desk drawer and pulled out a pack of unfiltered cigarettes. Then she took out a pair of reading glasses and put them on. She lit up and the smoke whirled around her head, staying steady in the still air. She smoothed the flannel bag and examined the sigils from all sides. "I know this work. It's by a voodoo lady by the name of Liliane."

"Where would I find her?" Bolan asked.

"Down by the docks," Calista replied. "She's got a little shop there. She's a bad one to go messing about with," the fortune teller went on. "We hear that she's tied up with Papa Glapion, and he's a man who lives with the dark side of the occult."

"What about zombies?" Bolan asked, thinking about what Escudo had said about his son being made into a zombie.

Calista hugged herself as if experiencing a chill. "They say he knows how to raise the dead. But they remember nothing about who they used to be. Mommas don't remember their children. Husbands don't know their wives. It's a very bad thing."

"Do you know where I would find him?"

"No, *cher*. He is a very dangerous man. Some say he can change shapes, like the werewolf, and that he drinks human blood on nights of the full moon." Calista picked up a Tarot deck and started shuffling the oversized cards. "Cut the deck. I will do a reading for you."

"Thanks, but I don't have time," Bolan replied.

She looked up at him. "Please. I sense a darkness following you. I want to know that it will stay with you and not be left here when you go."

Bolan cut the cards.

She gathered them up and began fanning them across the desktop. "You are a hunter," she said in a low voice, studying the cards as she turned them over. "You are here hunting a man, a very dangerous man. But it is not Papa Glapion. This man is a stranger from another country. Two women are involved. One, a dark lady with good in her heart but who walks her own path. The other one carries a black stone for a heart. You should fear this lady, because she will try to take your life." She paused, closing her eyes for a moment. "This man you are hunting, *cher,* he is at a place made of steel, surrounded by deep water." She glanced at the cards again. "I sense good fortune in the end, but there will be a cost. Whether you pay it, or someone close to you, I do not know.'' She held out her hand.

Bolan added another fifty to the one already on the desk.

THE BAYOU BAR Restaurant seemed efficient enough to do a fast turnover during the lunch hour, but it possessed the soul and decor of a speakeasy. The main bar was easily a hundred years old, as was the heavy cash register that sat on one end of the counter. A line of huge-bladed ceiling fans stirred the air. The walls were covered with prints, sheet music from classic jazz and blues pieces and signed photographs of King Oliver, Jelly Roll Morton and Louis Armstrong.

Bolan took a seat at the back of the main dining room near a pair of marble-based fountains. The restaurant was dark and the menu extensive. He took the special of the day and gave the waitress a twenty-dollar tip, saying that he wanted to have some time to enjoy the meal. She smiled at him and told him he could have all the time he needed.

The Executioner watched the crowd. He was dressed in charcoal pants, a red-and-black-striped pullover, hiking boots and a light vest that covered the Desert Eagle in a paddle holster at his back.

Dennis Wynnewood arrived just after noon. Bolan noticed that he looked nervous, handling the valise in his hand as if it was loaded with toxic chemicals. The hostess seated him at a table near the front of the restaurant.

Less than ten minutes later, a woman with blond hair cut in a punk style sat at his table. She talked animatedly for a short time, her eyes focused on the attorney.

Wynnewood slid the valise under the table to her, then he carefully looked around the room. The woman clearly understood the significance of his look, and Bolan saw her lean in to speak to the lawyer. Wynnewood's face turned white.

A tall dark-haired man approached the upright piano set back in the dim recesses of the restaurant. He sat at the keyboard and began to play a spirited jazz song. People started to move out onto the dance floor.

Bolan watched the blonde grab Wynnewood by the arm and hustled him toward the restaurant's side door. The lawyer didn't look like a man who was happy to go. The Executioner dropped money on the table to cover his check and got into motion. He noticed that three other men were also making their way to the side door. One of them was white, the other two Oriental.

They noticed Bolan, and one of the Orientals lagged behind, his hand up under his jacket. He stopped at the door after the others had gone through and turned to face him. He stuck a cigarette between his lips with his free hand. "Got a light?" he asked.

"Sure," Bolan replied. He reached down to his pants pocket as though going for a lighter, then brought his open palm rocketing up toward the man's face, catching him under the chin. The cigarette shredded against the guy's lips as his head thumped against the metal door. His gun clattered to the floor, and he sagged unconscious to the floor. The Executioner drew the Desert Eagle and stepped out the door, which opened onto a narrow alley.

Bolan saw the woman marching Wynnewood ahead of her at gunpoint, the valise held in her other hand. The two guns trailing her had their weapons out too, but they were a half second behind Bolan in their reaction time.

The Executioner leveled his .44 and dropped the sights over the first man, firing into the guy's chest from less than thirty feet. The 240-grain boattails sent the man crashing into a collection of metal trashcans, scattering a couple of scavenging alley cats.

The other man got off one shot that slammed into the door beside Bolan. The Executioner returned fire, the bullet catching the man in the throat and knocking him down, dead before he hit the ground.

The woman had responded by sprinting for a blue convertible that came screaming from the other end of the alley. She had started off by dragging Wynnewood after her, but had given that up. She took cover behind a wrought-iron overhang against a cinder-block wall that held hanging plants and flower boxes. Bolan caught a brief glimpse of an exposed thigh as she drew a pistol.

Wynnewood stood between the Executioner and the woman, seemingly frozen in place.

"Get down!" Bolan shouted at him.

The small pistol glinted in the woman's hand as she pointed it at Wynnewood.

Even though he didn't have a clear shot, Bolan loosed three rounds at her. None of them touched her, but they hit the hanging flowerpots, scattering soil and plants.

Bolan stripped the empty magazine from the Desert Eagle and recharged it as the convertible came to a screeching halt beside the woman. A gunner in the passenger seat unlimbered a MAC-10 and fired a burst that sent the Executioner diving for cover.

Shocked into action, Wynnewood ran toward Bolan, who saw the woman get up and level her pistol. There was no way Bolan could get off a clear shot. He intercepted Wynnewood, grabbing the man's jacket and shoving him up against the back wall of the restaurant.

The woman's pistol cracked.

Wynnewood stumbled and fell, at the same time pulling at Bolan. The warrior went with it, avoiding the ragged line of bullets from the MAC-10 that ripped cracks into the brickwork.

Throwing his arm out, Bolan snap-fired the .44 and punched holes in the convertible's windshield. The woman sprinted from her position, valise in hand and leaped into the back of the car.

"I've been shot," Wynnewood cried as Bolan yanked him to his feet by his jacket.

"Get up, or you're going to be dead." Bolan hustled the lawyer toward the restaurant's side exit. The convertible's engine roared as the vehicle lunged at him, dragging the bumper against the side of the alley and throwing sparks.

The gunner's MAC-10 cut loose again on full-auto, chopping holes through the metal of the door as Bolan pushed Wynnewood inside. He followed him in a distance-grabbing dive, setting the restaurant's patrons screaming.

Bolan got to his feet, the Desert Eagle tight in his fist. He checked Wynnewood and saw the man had been shot in the back of the thigh and the left buttock. Both wounds appeared to be superficial.

"I'm shot," Wynnewood said again, gazing fearfully at the blood as he lay on his side.

"You'll live," Bolan told him. He looked for the Oriental he'd knocked unconscious inside the restaurant. The guy was still lying facedown where he'd dropped him.

"Put down your gun," Bolan heard an authoritative voice say behind him.

He turned to face a thick-set man holding a pistol-grip shotgun aimed at his midsection.

"I'm an FBI agent," Bolan said. "Let me show you my ID."

"Slowly," the bouncer cautioned him.

Bolan did so, and the guy lowered the shotgun but didn't put it away. "Has anyone called the cops?"

"Yeah. They're on the way."

"Man," Wynnewood said, "they knew it was a trap. They knew they were being watched. How'd they know?"

Bolan didn't bother to explain. "Did you recognize any of them?"

"No."

"Not even the woman?"

"No! For Christ's sake, I'm bleeding to death here!"

Bolan ignored the whining. He had little sympathy for the lawyer. Wynnewood had placed himself on the firing line. Without the Executioner's help, the lawyer would have probably ended up dead.

He turned over the prone Oriental. The middle of his forehead sported a neat, round bullet hole.

"He's dead," a waitress said, her voice quavering with shock.

"Who shot him?" Bolan asked.

"The piano player."

He looked around, not really expecting to see the dark-haired man who'd been playing the piano. "Did you know him?"

"No."

"What about you?" Bolan asked the bouncer.

The man shook his head. "It was the first time he'd played here."

The Oriental's cohorts had obviously been unable to get him out in time, and it had been too dangerous to leave him behind to fall into police custody.

While the restaurant's management was busy with its clientele, Bolan left by the side exit, pausing only long enough to search the dead men. He found nothing helpful on either of them.

He quit the scene. The scream of police sirens was invading the neighborhood, and the crowd that had gathered had stopped traffic out in the main street. He still had leads to follow up.

LILIANE'S VOODOO SHOP was situated across the Mississippi River from the New Orleans Naval Support Activity. The sign advertising it offered fortunes, palm readings, charms and materials.

A bell over the multipaned door jangled when Bolan entered. A young Creole woman stood behind the high counter. The shelves around her held an assortment of books, bones and implements.

"Can I help you?" she asked.

"I'm here to see Liliane," Bolan replied.

"Do you have an appointment?" She took a leather-bound notebook from behind the counter and flipped through it.

"No. But this should get me one." Bolan held out his FBI ID.

The young woman didn't seem fazed. "Will she be needing a lawyer?"

"No."

She closed the appointment book firmly. "Then I don't see that she needs to be bothered with you."

Before Bolan could respond, an old woman's voice said, "It's all right, Celine. I'll see this man."

Liliane stood in the doorway at the rear of the shop, holding a curtain of beads out of the way. She was a little birdlike woman, from her thin frame and bowed shoulders to her raven hair, which she wore in a tight bun. She held a shawl around her shoulders. Her gaze was bright and hard.

Bolan gave her his FBI cover name.

She stared at him intently. "That is only who you call yourself now," she said. "You've worn many other names, but you are the hunter. Come." She beckoned him with a long-nailed finger.

Bolan followed Liliane through the bead-hung doorway and up a short flight of steps. She led him into a small, elegantly furnished living room, then waved him to an antique couch festooned with doilies.

"I knew you were coming," Liliane said, arranging herself in a rocking chair. A black cat with one white paw left his spot in the corner and jumped up into her lap.

Bolan remained standing. "Then you know why I'm here."

The old woman absently stroked the cat. "No. I heard you were looking for me from the people on the street. Madame Calista often talks about the fortunes she tells other people. Today, she talked about you."

Taking the gris-gris bag from his pocket, Bolan handed it to her.

"I made this one," Liliane said, smoothing it flat against her palm.

"Do you remember who you made it for?"

"No."

Bolan took a mug shot of the man from a pocket in his vest and handed it to her. "Do you recognize this man?"

She studied the picture. "Yes, I do."

"I've been told he works for someone named Papa Glapion."

Liliane handed the mug shot back. "What do you know of this *bokor?*"

"People seem to be afraid of him."

"But you are not?" Liliane asked.

Bolan shook his head. "No. I understand that Glapion is dangerous, but I'm not afraid of him."

"Then you are not a very wise man," the old woman said. "Papa Glapion has the power, the *real* power, to make the dead rise and walk. I have seen him do this. He has cast his spell on people, struck them dead and had them buried out in the bayous, then made them claw their way up out of their own graves."

"I need to know where I can find him," Bolan said.

"You'll go hunting your own death then," Liliane replied. "And it might not stop with that. You could lose your soul to him and become a zombie."

"He's working with a man who's responsible for many deaths in this city. This morning an eleven-year-old boy was hurt by these people. They cut him open, took part of him out and left him in the swamp to die. I can't walk away from that," Bolan replied.

She kept silent for a time. "How old do you think I am?" she asked finally.

"I don't know."

"I'm eighty-three, hunter, old enough to be your grandmother. When I was a girl, maybe nine, maybe ten, Papa Glapion's father, who was also a *bokor*, cast a spell on me. I was spying on him. I wanted to learn about the voodoo, so I followed him and saw him conduct some rituals. When he caught me, he was very angry. This spell he wove took part of my soul away from me. When I die, my soul will be trapped, never knowing any rest. On his deathbed, he gave the secret of the curse to his son. I have had to do Papa Glapion's bidding ever since."

Bolan waited patiently while Liliane mopped at the tears that had gathered in her eyes.

"Celine is my great-granddaughter," she went on, "and I need to see that she's protected from the *bokor* before I die. He desires her very much." She shook her fist at him. "I sense in you a very strong power, but I do not know if it will be enough against the *bokor*. Still, I must risk this to keep Celine free."

Suddenly aware of a movement behind him, Bolan turned, dropping his hand to the butt of the Desert Eagle.

Three men stood in the doorway. Their clothes were ripped. Their eyes were glazed, reminding Bolan of junkies riding out a dose of PCP. The odor of damp, moldering earth clung to them, thick and sweet. They held machetes.

"Papa Glapion knows," Liliane gasped, shoving herself out of her chair. "The *bokor* knows you came to talk to me."

The Executioner lifted the .44 and pointed it at the leader as the three men shambled forward. They ignored him and kept moving on. Bolan squeezed the trigger, aiming the round at the man's upper arm.

The impact caused the man to stagger back, and he screamed in an almost inhuman voice. Raising the machete, he lunged at Bolan, blood streaming down his arm.

"They are zombies!" Liliane shrieked, holding her hands before her eyes. The cat streaked from the room. "You cannot kill them!"

The machete went whistling by his head, as the Executioner ducked. He then stepped to one side and slammed his free foot against the man's knee. Bone cracked, and his attacker dropped to the ground.

The second man was less than three feet away from the Desert Eagle's muzzle when Bolan fired again. The 240-grain hollowpoint caught the man between the eyes and blew out the back of his head.

The warrior saw the floored attacker scrabbling across the carpet toward Liliane, his machete still gripped in his hand. The old woman stood, frozen, against the far wall.

With the third man almost upon him, Bolan dropped the .44's sights over the crippled attacker, then squeezed the trigger. The bullets hit him in the back of the head and the neck, severing his spinal cord.

The third man launched himself at Bolan, screaming incoherently.

Driven forward by the man's weight, Bolan and his adversary went hurtling through the window. The Executioner hit the wood-shingled roof hard, his attacker on top of him. He managed to grab the man's machete-wielding hand, but the effort started them sliding down the slope of the roof.

They hung at the edge for just a moment. Bolan tried to bring up the pistol, but then gravity pulled them over the edge. Bolan twisted in midair, barely coming around in time to land on a vendor's pushcart, snapping the wheels off the axle.

The Executioner stood up amid the wreckage of the pushcart and watched as the staggering behemoth got to his feet—having landed in the street—and looked around for his machete.

"Don't," Bolan warned, raising the Desert Eagle.

"You must die!" the man screamed. His hand closed around the haft of the machete. A horn suddenly blared, then a taxi slammed into the man, pinning him between its hood and an oncoming pickup truck. The two vehicles came to a rest in the center of the street.

Bolan walked toward the vehicles, still holding his Desert Eagle. He looked down at the man and saw that he'd nearly been cut in two by the collision. Blood pooled under the cars' bumpers.

"I didn't see him," the taxi driver said. "One minute the street was clear, then there he was. It's not my fault."

"Ain't nothing gonna live through that," the pickup driver said. "The poor bastard came close to being twins."

Bolan knelt and reached through the maze of torn flesh and twisted metal until he could get to the man's pants pockets. There was no ID on him, nothing to indicate who he might have been.

"He was a zombie."

Bolan turned and found Liliane standing a few feet away, Celine beside her. A crowd of onlookers had gathered behind them.

"They will not be the last that the *bokor* sends after you. He knows you are a danger to him," the old woman said.

"Tell me where to find him."

Liliane stepped closer. "Death Adder Lagoon. Maybe you will find him there."

Bolan couldn't recall seeing that name on the maps he had. He also knew that many of the bayou areas weren't marked, familiar only to the locals who lived there. "How will I find it?"

The old woman handed him a gris-gris made of doeskin. "Here. I have drawn a map as well as I remember. I haven't been there since my soul was stolen away by Glapion's father.

"Also, I have made some of my best magic and put it in that bag." She looked up at him. "I have waited for a champion for a long time." She folded his hand over the gris-gris. "Please don't let me down."

"I'll find him," Bolan said. He leathered the Desert Eagle and walked away. No one tried to stop him.

BOLAN RENTED A MOTEL ROOM long enough to manage a shower, a change of clothes, a meal and a phone call to update the Stony Man Farm intel support group. By 3:10 p.m. he was back on the road. The other meet Wynnewood had set up was scheduled to take place at 4:00 p.m., at the Chalmette National Historical Park. Bolan planned to arrive no later than 3:30 and do a brief recon.

He punched in the number for Eduard Hamlin on the car phone. As he listened to it ring, he shifted in the contoured seat, trying to get more comfortable. The fall from the second-floor window had racked up an impressive amount of bruises and sore muscles. The police scanner had been full of the attack, but specific details had been meager. The radio and television news hinted that an FBI agent might have been involved, and that a witness had turned up regarding the Carrion Killings.

Bolan didn't know how much longer his cover would hold, but he couldn't worry about it too much. For now, it was enough to be Special Agent Travis Fox and stay out of jail.

"Hamlin." The black-market kingpin sounded tense.

"What have you found out?" Bolan asked, following the highway. Chalmette Park was less than a mile away.

"The guy you're looking for is hooked up with some local witch doctor named Glapion."

"I knew that. Tell me something I don't know."

"This is going to take some time."

"I'm late in checking back with you as it is," Bolan pointed out. "How much time do you think you're going to need?"

"It's hard to say. These guys have dug in pretty deep in the local scene."

"Find out everything you can about the different kinds of transportation," Bolan ordered. His own conversation with Kurtzman at the Farm had been unproductive. According to the cybernetics specialist, no licenses had been issued to new courier services at any of the public or privately owned airfields, and no existing courier services had changed hands in the past year. "These people have to be flying in and out of the city in jets. There's no other way they can make delivery with the deadlines they're working against."

"I've got teams canvassing the airports now. I should know something soon."

"I'll be in touch." Bolan broke the connection. He turned over the information he had so far in his mind. The organ harvesters had no alternative means of ferrying body parts around in the time allowed. They had to do it by jet. So he didn't understand why a lead hadn't surfaced. Getting to the next available major airport in Baton Rouge would add another two hours at least to ground travel time. Anyplace smaller would leave them too open to discovery. It had to be someplace where they could fit in.

He was also certain that the transportation support for the organ brokers was located in one of New Orleans's major airports. The answers were there; it was just a matter of asking the right questions.

Opening the doeskin gris-gris Liliane had given him, Bolan took out the hand-drawn map folded inside. So far, he hadn't been able to match the drawing with any of the maps he had, or with the notes in his warbook. It depicted a small grove in a maze of bayous. He knew that without a guide of some kind he could search for hours and never find it. He refolded the map and put it back in the bag.

He stopped in the park's public parking area and got out. Dressed in jeans, running shoes and a New Orleans Saints jersey, he fit in easily with the park-goers. He opened the trunk of the Stealth and took out a tan duster and a Neostead bullpup shotgun on a Whipit sling. He put on the sling, then covered it with the duster. He placed extra shells for the weapon in the duster pockets. He carried the Desert Eagle in shoulder leather.

He closed the trunk and moved off to start his recon.

## 7

As it turned out, Abe Dreyser didn't have a mistress. Checks into his credit-card account revealed that he had been frequenting a restaurant that had a large homosexual clientele.

Arne Madigan led the way into the restaurant, Kaliope bringing up the rear. "Are you sure Dreyser's medical records are up-to-date?" he asked her. "There was already a screw up with his routine activities, and we can't afford to make mistakes."

"Yes," Kaliope said. "He's clean."

Madigan spotted Dreyser, seated in a booth.

The organ dealer stopped at the table and put on a polite face that masked his irritation with the situation. "Mr. Dreyser?" he said, and flashed an ID.

"Detective Kline, NOPD. I'm afraid I've got some bad news."

"Bad news?" Dreyser repeated, clearly alarmed enough not to question how they'd known of his whereabouts.

"About your wife. If you'll come with us, sir, we'll take you to her."

"Of course." Dreyser stood shakily.

Madigan took Dreyser's elbow and guided him out the front door of the restaurant, Kaliope following them.

Out in the parking lot, Madigan turned to him. "Let my partner drive your car over for you. We'll get there quicker in my vehicle."

"Thanks." Dreyser dropped his keys into Kaliope's waiting palm. He pointed to a row of cars parked against the curb. "It's the light blue one."

Madigan led Dreyser to a Lincoln Continental parked behind the restaurant. The driver got out and opened the door for them. Dr. Winston Chen, already dressed in surgeon's blues, sat in the back of the car, his black bag beside him.

Dreyser got in first, then Madigan took his seat. He rapped on the glass partition, letting the driver know they were ready. The Lincoln powered up smoothly.

"Hey, this isn't a police car," Dreyser said, suspicion beginning to dawn on him after his initial shock. "What the hell is going on here?"

"Shut up," Madigan ordered. He glanced at his watch, then at Chen. "We need to be in the air no later than 3:30."

"I can do it," Chen replied.

"What's going on?" Dreyser yelped. "Who are you?"

Ignoring his distress, Madigan slipped a $CO_2$ dart gun from inside his jacket and plunged a dart into Dreyser's thigh, close to the groin.

The man screamed and stared fearfully at the narcodart sticking out of his leg.

Then his eyes rolled up in his head and he passed out.

Withdrawing a box from under the seat, Madigan took out a hospital orderly's uniform. He stripped out of his suit and put on the uniform. As he completed his dress, the car's phone rang.

"I'm proceeding with the meet at Chalmette Park," Kaliope said on the other end.

"If things seem too dicey, don't take the chance," Madigan said. "You're worth much more to me alive than you are dead."

"Of course."

Ten minutes later, Madigan and Chen transferred the unconscious Dreyser to the back of an ambulance that had been waiting for them on a side road only a few blocks from Touro Infirmary. They strapped Dreyser onto the gurney, and Chen started prepping him for surgery, giving orders to the ambulance team.

"I'm not going to screw around with this harvest," Chen said as they rocketed into the hospital's emergency zone. "They're going to get a transplantable organ."

Madigan nodded. He grabbed one side of the gurney and helped shove it out the doors when they were opened. An orderly met them as they hit the ground.

"I've got a man here in full cardiac arrest," Chen yelled. "He hasn't responded to CPR. I need an OR now."

Madigan kept the gurney moving as the orderly ran ahead of them. "Stat! We've got a code-blue!" His shouts summoned a doctor, who joined Madigan, Chen and their original ambulance team in the elevator.

"How long has he been down?" the doctor asked, pulling Dreyser's lid back and shining a penlight into his eye. "Hey, this guy's breathing."

Madigan slid his silenced Detonics .451 from under his shirt and shoved it into the man's face. "You won't be if you say another word. Get us into that OR with no problems, and you get to live."

Inside the OR, Dreyser was placed on the operating table. Chen went to work on his breastbone with a surgical saw, then used the chest spreader. Dreyser's ribs snapped as Chen cracked the man open to reveal the beating heart. Not long afterward, the heart was packed in ice in a chest.

Then Madigan shot the doctor. The man had known it was coming and had tried to back away, but the organ dealer shot him through the head, then stepped over his body on his way to the door.

They were almost through the ER when the alarm sounded. A security guard at the door went for his gun.

Madigan swept up the Detonics and fired, placing his round directly between the man's eyes.

The ambulance was waiting for them out in the parking lot. Less than a mile from the hospital, they abandoned the vehicle in an alley and were picked up by a van and a late-model Ford sedan.

Within minutes, the ice chest with Abe Dreyser's very expensive AB-negative heart was on its way to New Orleans International Airport.

Madigan checked his watch and saw that it was almost time for Kaliope's meeting at the park. He decided to go there, as well. He always liked to see Kaliope at work.


"DAMN!"

Marisa Ayshe jumped when she heard Lockspur's voice come over the frequency they were using for the undercover operation. She stood in the park grounds near the top of a levee overlooking the Mississippi River. "What?"

"The bastards have hit again," the homicide captain said. "They took a guy into Touro Infirmary and chopped his heart out just a few minutes ago." He gave her the rest of the story that was just breaking across police communications.

Ayshe shivered. Now one more victim had been added to the already long string of bodies.

"Marisa?" Lockspur said.

She looked out over the slow rolling length of the river, then tapped the transmit button. "I'm here."

"Are you okay?"

"Yes."

The homicide captain hesitated. "We can pull the plug on this thing now. Just close up shop and go home. We know we're running a bigger risk than we signed up for."

Ayshe looked over at the Visitor Center and the National Cemetery where Lockspur was hidden with seven other men. "No. We're here to get a job done, so let's do it."

"That's the way," Lockspur said encouragingly. "We'll get this sting wrapped up this afternoon and be home to get a good night's sleep."

Unfortunately Ayshe knew that wasn't true. If they managed to bust the front people who came for the money stashed in the briefcase she held at her side, they were only a link that would lead them back along the chain to the people behind the Carrion Killings.

She studied the storm clouds gathering overhead and felt the increased humidity.

"Miss Harper?"

Upon hearing her cover name, Ayshe turned. "Yes," she said, tightening her grip on the briefcase.

The man was pale and seemed unfamiliar with the New Orleans climate. He wore an unbuttoned trench coat over a turtleneck and pants. "I think you have something for me," he said. He mopped the back of his neck with a handkerchief, his arm movement revealing the pistol stuck in his waistband.

"How do I know who you are?" Ayshe responded.

The man made a show of looking around, then faced her again. "I don't see anyone else out here putting the arm on you for one hundred thousand dollars." He held out his hand.

"Contact," Lockspur said into the concealed earphone Ayshe wore. "Let him have it."

Ayshe lifted the briefcase, hoping the surveillance team would be closing in at that moment, as they'd planned. She rested her free hand on her hip, near the Glock.

The man took the briefcase and tossed her a jaunty salute. He began to walk away.

"We'll take him," Lockspur said into her earphone. In the distance, she could see the plainclothes detectives start to close in.

A rifle shot split the air, and one of the plainclothes detectives went down.

"Dammit!" Lockspur yelled. "Get clear and watch your asses out there!"

Ayshe knew they'd been set up. She reached behind her and pulled out the Glock. Fifty yards away, the man spun, his gun in his hand. Ayshe took a two-handed grip on her side arm and squeezed the trigger. Even with all the noise and confusion going on around her, she was surprised at how aware she was of the Glock's detonation and the way it jumped in her hands.

Over her gunsight, she saw the man go down, his gun sailing away from him. Behind her, three off-road equipped pickups started to race across the park grounds. But her attention remained fixed on the man she'd shot.

"Marisa!" Lockspur yelled.

Rifle shots cracked around her from the hidden snipers. Ayshe stood rooted to the spot.

"Dammit, Ayshe, move or I'll shoot you myself!"

Lockspur's voice finally penetrated her senses and she broke into a stumbling run. She reached the prone man, and trying to ignore the bloody splotches across his chest, she knelt down to pick up the briefcase lying beside him.

She looked up to see one of the off-road pickups careering down on her from less than thirty yards away. She knew she wasn't going to get away before it ran her down.

Then a tall man was beside her, grabbing her elbow and yanking her up. Ayshe just had time to realize it was the FBI agent, Fox, before his shotgun blasted into action.

A pattern of holes appeared across the pickup's windshield. The driver veered sharply, the bumper missing Ayshe by inches.

"Run!" the big man shouted, pumping his weapon. He fired twice more, scoring both times on the pickup's cab.

Ayshe ran as hard as she could, the heavy briefcase weighing her down. In front of them, the pickup's oversized tires tore up the ground as it braked and swung back around in their direction.

She started to slow down, but a firm hand on her shoulder propelled her forward.

"If you stop, you're dead," Bolan said. "Break right when I tell you to."

Ayshe wondered if she'd made the jump from the frying pan into the fire. Everyone around the man seemed to get real dead, real quick.

"Break!" he commanded.

She streaked toward the tree line bordering the levee, hoping she wasn't making a mistake.

THE EXECUTIONER RAISED the Neostead combat shotgun to his shoulder and took aim at the oncoming pickup. The South African 12-gauge held a dozen rounds in twin magazines along the top of the weapon. With the bullpup design, when he racked the slide forward, it cleared the spent shell underneath, then chambered the next.

Bullets from the cab ran a ragged line across the ground beside the warrior. With the shotgun held snug against his shoulder, he fired. The round exploded through the center of the windshield, leaving a gaping hole. Bolan threw himself to one side, and the pickup went grinding past him.

He got to his feet. After racking the slide of his weapon, he launched into pursuit of the vehicle.

As the pickup came around in a tight turn, the Executioner vaulted onto the chrome running board and grabbed the roll bar extending over the cab. The guy on the passenger side brought up his CAR-15, his initial burst blowing away the side mirror.

Broken glass stung Bolan's hand. He aimed at the passenger, then pulled the trigger.

"You son of a bitch!" the driver yelled. He began to fire wildly at the Executioner with a small automatic.

Bolan wrapped his hand around the Neostead's buttstock, then drove it hard through the broken windshield, aiming for the driver's skull. The abbreviated muzzle splintered the man's head. The pickup began to veer out of control, plunging through the brush.

The soldier pulled open the door, dragged the dead driver out, then swung into the cab. Working the wheel fiercely, he steered the pickup down the incline off the levee and out into the clearing.

Ground troops had now joined the other two pickups, and Bolan could count at least three bodies littering the ground.

Scanning the area, Bolan spotted the detective among the trees at the edge of the clearing. In the dossier that Brognola had sent to cover the mission, Kurtzman had included brief files on the homicide detectives involved with the Carrion Killings. Bolan had learned that the woman's name was Marisa Ayshe.

He had shifted gears and pinned the accelerator to the floor when he saw one of the remaining pickups racing toward Ayshe. A shooter hung out of the passenger-side window, an Uzi in his fists. Bolan closed in as he watched Ayshe return fire sporadically, seeking new cover in the tree line. Branches and leaves tumbled down after her.

The driver spotted the Executioner coming at him too late. At the last minute, Bolan cut the wheel hard and smashed broadside into the front of the other vehicle. The impact flung the driver into the door with bruising force.

Recovering quickly, the soldier drew the Desert Eagle from shoulder leather and fired from point-blank range. The bullet starred the windshield and hammered through the man's forehead. Bolan charged out of the pickup, his combat shotgun at the ready.

The other man from the pickup had survived the crash and was scrambling into the brush. He spotted Bolan and came around quickly, bringing up his Uzi. Before the Executioner could bring his Neostead into play, Ayshe stepped out of the trees and fired a double-tap that caught the man in the chest and punched him backward.

"Thanks," Bolan said.

A thin line of blood from a scratch marked the woman's cheek. She kept both hands on her pistol as she looked at him. "I guess I owed you one."

"Maybe." Bolan searched the battlefield. Ground troops were rushing toward their position. He checked out the other pickup. A sliding rack projected from under the seat. A Mossberg 500 shotgun and an M-14 rifle occupied the slots. "Have you got a radio?"

"It has only limited access," Ayshe said as she took up a position on the nose of the pickup. She fired a trio of shots at the approaching group of men. "Lockspur has the main radio."

Bolan found a cache of clips for the rifle and extra rounds for the shotgun in a plastic box at the end of the sliding rack. He slipped three magazines of 7.62 mm ammunition into his duster pocket and picked up the M-14. "Do you know if he radioed in for help?"

"No. I'm set up for the tach channel only."

Bullets suddenly thudded into the side of the pickup that sheltered them, shattering the glass in the windows.

Bolan wheeled to the other side of the cab and pulled the M-14 to his shoulder. He peered down the open sights, located his first target and fired a pair of shots. The rounds took the man high on the left side of his chest. The gunner spun and dropped. The Executioner mentally tagged his next three targets, then he squeezed the trigger as he rolled across the trio of gunners. The first two went down with head shots, and the third took two bullets in the chest.

"Who *are* these guys?" Ayshe gasped as she shoved a fresh magazine into her pistol.

"I don't know yet."

"So how did you know to be here?" Her face was tight with concentration.

"Through Dennis Wynnewood." Bolan fell silent, homing in on a gunner who'd sprinted from behind a tree, trying to cut the distance to their holding position. When he had the man bracketed, Bolan pulled the trigger. The heavy 7.62 mm round caught him full in the face and drove him two steps backward before he collapsed.

"But he didn't know I was a cop," Ayshe said.

"That's right," Bolan agreed.

"Did you know I was going to be here?" Ayshe asked.

"No. I thought I was going to get a look at a transaction between these people and one of their clients."

Bullets suddenly skipped across the side of the pickup bed only inches from Bolan, ripping into the metal. He ducked, but not before he caught a glimpse of a blond-haired woman positioned on a rise less than a hundred yards away.

Ayshe continued their dialogue, anger apparent in her voice. "So then you gave me away when you jumped Wynnewood."

Bolan looked at her. "You were already burned. There's no way they would have let you, Lockspur and the rest of your team get away alive.''

"How did you know I was a cop?"

"I saw Lockspur signal you at the hospital this morning."

Bolan cut their conversation short as a gunner stepped out from behind his cover, a grenade in his hand. The Executioner fired three rapid shots that knocked the man to the ground, but not before he'd succeeded in lobbing the missile.

Moving quickly, the big man grabbed Ayshe and shoved her deeper into the tree line. "Grenade! Move!"

She ran, plowing her way through the brush.

Bolan followed. They were almost twenty yards away when the grenade went off. The concussive wave washed over them, and shrapnel cut the foliage from the trees.

Sirens screamed across the park, and NOPD patrol cars roared out onto the battlefield. A helicopter could be seen approaching in the distance. The gun crew gave ground rapidly, disappearing into the trees.

Ayshe stared at Bolan. "You're not an FBI agent, are you?"

"No."

"Then who?"

"Just someone involved in justice."

"That's as cryptic as hell."

Bolan shrugged. "Maybe, but it's the truth." Glancing through the trees, he saw Lockspur and two uniforms jogging toward the tree line.

"What happens now?" Ayshe asked him.

"I walk away."

"Just like that."

He nodded. "Just like that."

"What if I don't let you?" She waggled her pistol meaningfully at him.

Turning, Bolan started to walk away. "Then you get to shoot me in the back," he said over his shoulder.

"Dammit, Fox, come back here."

Bolan stopped, then turned and looked at her. "These people have to be stopped, and the police aren't going to be able to do it with their methods. I can. But part of this leads out into the bayou." He paused. "I need a guide, and you were born in the area." He watched her digest his suggestion.

"Do you think you have a lead on these people?" she finally asked.

"Yeah, and it starts with Papa Glapion." Bolan began to walk, Ayshe falling into step beside him. "But he's not the guy handling the organ brokering. Someone else has the connections."

"We haven't been able to trace Glapion," Ayshe said.

"I think I know where he is," the Executioner replied. "If it checks out, I've got the location of his *hounfour*."

"What's his part in this?"

"You saw the boy this morning."

She nodded.

"And you know about zombie powder."

"Yes."

"One of the biggest problems with organ harvesting is time," Bolan said. They came within sight of his car, the sounds of the police units behind them growing fainter. "Using Glapion's skills, whoever's behind the organ theft ring could start holding the victims longer, without fear of the victims escaping, and exposing their base of operations. Also, in their drugged state, they can be held for days."

"If I go with you," Ayshe said, "I could be putting my job on the line, because Lockspur's not going to like getting cut out of the loop.''

Bolan didn't say anything. The decision had to be hers.

"But if Glapion's involved, these people could start harvesting more organs out in the bayous,'' she went on thoughtfully. "They'll have his contacts and resources. It'll be harder to catch them.'' Her voice lowered. "And those are my people.''

Bolan unlocked the car door and popped the latch.

Ayshe slid into the back seat, noting the computer in the front. "Let's go,'' she said, "before we get caught.''

Bolan eased the sports car out of the parking area just as the heavens opened and the rain started to fall.

**8**

"How bad is it?" Arne Madigan asked. He stood in the center of the suite of offices he maintained in New Orleans's Garden District and focused on the television in the elegant entertainment center that filled the opposite wall.

"We lost four of our people," Kaliope said. "I had to shoot one myself when I realized we weren't going to be able to transport him out." She lounged on an antique couch upholstered in green satin. "The rest were Glapion's crew and some of the local talent we picked up."

Madigan studied the scenes on the television. Reporters and camera crews swarmed over the Chalmette National Historical Park. He used the remote control to flip through the local channels. They were all covering the same news item.

"They can't be tied back to us?" Madigan asked.

"Not directly to our operation," the woman answered. "If someone gets into the right files, they can be traced back to Hong Kong and then possibly to us, but whoever it was would have to have a hell of a database and more reach than the NOPD or the FBI."

Madigan had known from the beginning that the organ-harvesting operation wouldn't remain in the shadows of the city for long. But that FBI agent, Travis Fox, was setting off alarms that Madigan couldn't afford to ignore. "What about the FBI agent, Fox?" he asked.

"He was there," Kaliope replied. "Then he disappeared. From what our informant inside the PD tells me, that homicide captain, Lockspur, is pretty keen to know where he is, too. Also, one of their detectives is missing."

"Who?"

"Marisa Ayshe."

The name didn't ring any bells with Madigan.

"She was the woman who set up the buy through Wynnewood," Kaliope explained.

"Is there anything to show that she and Fox are linked?" Madigan asked.

"No."

"But it was Fox who coerced Wynnewood into setting up a buy with us?"

Kaliope nodded. "Fox has managed to get involved in every incident. There's more to him than meets the eye."

Madigan felt that, too. He'd been chased over the years by some of the best predators and law-enforcement agencies in the world. Fox felt like none of those and more like some kind of elemental force. Uncertainty surfaced in the back of his mind for the first time in a number of years. "What do they think happened to the detective?"

"Apparently Lockspur thinks she went with Fox."

"Why?"

"She has something the other detectives don't have," Kaliope replied. "Ayshe was raised in the bayou country."

"So Fox needs her to guide him," Madigan said thoughtfully. "Maybe we should have investigated Glapion further."

"We covered him as best as we could and turned up nothing that suggested we couldn't work with him," Kaliope said. "And so far the police haven't found anything that could link Glapion to our business. If they had, we'd have heard."

"But what if Fox has found a link?"

"Then why hasn't he turned it over to the NOPD?" Kaliope asked.

Madigan crossed the room to the computer on the big mahogany desk. He called up the Caribbean bank account he'd used for the Dreyser transaction. He saw that the money for the heart had been logged in. "Because he knows we've breached police security. One way or another." He brought up another screen that showed the anticipated acquisitions that Chen and his medical team would be harvesting the following day. Some of Chen's people had been quietly making selections of bayou residents, people that the *bokor*'s men were even now kidnapping. Then they would be able to lie back for a few weeks, giving their pursuers time to lose their edge.

"Do you think he's got a federal team waiting to act on this?" Kaliope asked.

Madigan switched off the computer. "I can't see a federal agency fielding a large unit that can react as quickly as he can."

"Possibly a small, covert team, then."

Madigan stood and looked out the window, his hands in his pockets. "Even if they do find us, they'll just be coming to their own deaths. Out there in those swamps, Glapion's people will be deadly." He smiled. "And our own teams aren't unused to such an environment. If this man is stupid enough to go looking there for us—assuming that he has made the connection to Glapion and knows where to find the man—he won't leave those bayous alive."

"He was very effective today," Kaliope said.

"You sound as though you admire him."

She raised her brows. "I do. He's the kind of man that a woman would be proud to let claim her—strong, bold, and with a certain dark, deadly edge." She licked her lips. "Actually I think you admire him, too."

"I like a strong adversary. It'll make me feel good to conquer him."

"If you're able," she taunted him.

Madigan grinned. "What if you had him in your sights?"

"I'd make sure it was a head shot," Kaliope replied coolly. "A man like that has to have a healthy heart. And I've never let lust come between me and profit.''

Madigan reached for his long coat and pulled it on. "When Chen removes Fox's heart, you'll be able to experience it first hand.''

MARISA AYSHE PEERED OUT the curtained window in her grandmother's kitchen. She'd taken the time to dress more warmly, knowing they'd be out in the bayous soon. She wore flannel long johns under her jeans, a turtleneck, and a thick cotton plaid shirt over it. Her pants were tucked into waterproof hiking boots.

Out in the yard, a dim glow from the computer screen in the FBI agent's sports car revealed his presence.

"That's not polite, *cher,*" Marie Desermeaux admonished Ayshe. She stood at the old wood-burning stove and stirred the contents of the iron pots. The smell of fresh fried *couche-couche,* red *boudin,* and blackbird-and-quail gumbo pervaded the kitchen.

"I know," Ayshe replied, "but I'm trying to fathom out this man.''

"Yet you are willing to go with him when he asked,'' her grandmother pointed out.

"He has information that I need."

"You still don't have to go with him. You could have him pass the information on to your boss, that Captain Lockspur."

"Fox wouldn't do that," Ayshe said. She dropped the curtain and turned from the window.

"Because he's afraid those men you're after would find out?"

"Yes." Ayshe filched some okra from the gumbo. Despite the tension of the day and the future uncertainty, she was ravenous. Fox seemed to have his feelings under control, which made Ayshe even more curious about him. What kind of man could deal with such danger and violence and not show signs of stress?

"What do you think of him?" she asked her grandmother.

For once, the old woman seemed cautious about giving her opinion.

Her grandmother looked at her and pulled at her left earlobe, a gesture that Ayshe knew meant she was troubled. "Basically, *cher,* I think that he is a good man. But he walks with death. This man knows death like it was his own mother. Once, maybe, he was like other men. But this mark has been with him for a long time. It seems to me that he has come to accept it, and to use it as a source of strength."

Ayshe laughed, trying to lighten the mood. "You sound like you did when I was a little girl, when you told me that the *loup-garou* could tell his future victims by the marks he saw on their palms. I know there are no were-wolves now."

Her grandmother's features became reproving. "Don't be so quick to dismiss such things, *cher*. Don't you and this man hope to find a *bokor*, a maker of zombies, tonight?"

"I'm sorry, Grandmère. I didn't mean to sound flippant."

The old woman waved away her apology. She began to ladle out big bowls of gumbo.

"This man, Fox, he is a good man," her grandmother said, "but a lonely one, as well. He's built walls that I doubt anyone will ever get through."

"I don't think he's a cop though, federal or otherwise," Ayshe said.

"He's a warrior," Desermeaux answered. "He knows caution, but he doesn't know fear. He knows life and will fight to protect, but he'll never know peace." She shook her head.

"He's not a man I'd want you to give your heart to."

"Don't worry, I don't think that's going to happen," Ayshe said, going back to her vigil at the window. "I tried that once, remember?"

"Yes, and as I recall, I told you that you should have married a man, not a boy."

It was an old argument, and not one that Ayshe wanted to go through again. She changed the subject. "Tell me about Death Adder Lagoon." Earlier, when the FBI agent had asked her grandmother about it, the old woman had appeared visibly shaken.

"That is a dark place, *cher,* and I fear for you. Great evils have always been committed there. People have lost their souls in that place. For as long as anyone in our family can remember, Death Adder Lagoon has been a place of power for the Glapions. It's no longer called Death Adder Lagoon, and I'm not sure its new name is listed on any map. I can find it for you, but are you sure you have to go there?"

Ayshe looked out the window again. "He is, and right now he knows more than I do."

"I'VE GOT A TENTATIVE ID on one of the people who killed Abe Dreyser in Touro Infirmary," Hal Brognola said.

Mack Bolan used the hands-free operation on the cellular phone. Out of range of conventional phone towers, he'd hooked into the LST-5C satellite transceiver he carried with him. He'd unfolded it on the Stealth's roof, and the communications frequency was clear despite the isolation of his surroundings.

"His name," the head Fed continued, "is Arne Madigan."

Bolan's computer monitor showed a dark-haired man in his early forties.

"He's as slick as they come, Striker. He's never done time for any of his crimes, either under his real name or the aliases he's used."

The attached fax machine rolled out sheets that gave more detailed information about Madigan's past, as Brognola continued to fill Bolan in.

"When we contacted people in Hong Kong, Madigan's last base," Brognola said, "they told us he'd been running a similar operation over there, bootlegging illegal organs."

"So then Madigan came here to open a new market," Bolan suggested.

"We think so. The authorities were about to close him down in Hong Kong, in spite of the hush money he was paying."

Bolan digested that. "He had to have brought a staff with him."

"Yeah, medical people, support teams and Intelligence guys."

"That's a lot of people to hide."

"Somewhere, Striker," the head Fed said, "Madigan's got to have found a nice hole to set up his operation. A warehouse, a building, someplace big."

Bolan figured it the same way. "What about known associates?"

The monitor brought up an Asian man with glasses, a receding hairline and a weak chin. "That's Dr. Winston Chen," Brognola explained. "Hong Kong believes he was the main surgeon working with Madigan, but they couldn't prove it. Despite their investigations, the guy came out squeaky clean." Bolan recognized the woman with the blond hair that now showed on the screen. "The lady's name is Kaliope. No last name. We don't know if that's her real name or an alias. There's no paperwork on her except for an eighteen-month stay in a psychiatric hospital in Greece.

She was involved in some political assassinations by a group of terrorists, but she was judged incompetent to stand trial. Five years ago, she escaped from the hospital, leaving behind her a dead orderly and two patients who are handicapped for life. She's dangerous, Striker.''

Bolan knew that. He'd already seen her in action.

More pictures followed, but the soldier recognized only one from the assault at Chalmette National Historic Park.

He tagged it, then told Brognola, ''Check on this one. I think you're going to find him in a New Orleans morgue.''

''I will.''

''What about the transportation angle?''

''Been there and back again, buddy. Aaron can't find any new businesses that specialize in courier service.''

''It's out there somewhere.''

''We'll find it.''

Closing the notebook computer, Bolan looked out at the stars through the branches of the cypress trees. ''I'll be in touch when I can.'' He'd already briefed the big Fed on the night's excursion.

"Stay hard out there, guy," Brognola said.

"I will." Bolan broke the connection and got out of the car. The night air felt clean, and it cleared some of the fatigue he felt from running too long without sleep.

The soldier got his duffel bag from the trunk and headed for the house. He scuffed his feet on the mat in front of the door and knocked.

Ayshe came to the door. "Come in. My grandmother has supper on the table."

Bolan started to protest, but the woman smiled as she looked up at him. "You can try to get out of it, but I have to warn you—generations of the Desermeaux family and friends have failed to get away from one of my grandmother's meals. She's managed to have them delay going to fight in the Second World War, the Korean War, the Vietnam War and the Gulf War. It you want to try your luck, go ahead."

Bolan followed her into the kitchen and smelled the food. "I think I'll take your advice." The night was going to stretch long, cold and hard ahead of them. A good meal would help stave off all three.

By the time they'd finished eating, the sounds of the bayou's nocturnal life filled the air.

The Executioner retreated to the bathroom long enough to manage a quick shower and a change of clothes. When he reemerged, he was dressed in his combat blacksuit and field boots. For the time being, he kept his guns in the duffel bag.

When he returned to the kitchen, he found Marie Desermeaux bent over the sink retching, while her granddaughter supported her.

"It's okay," Ayshe said over her shoulder to Bolan. "Leave us alone. Please." Her face had paled.

"Let me know if I can help." Bolan took his duffel bag and went out to the front yard. He settled the Desert Eagle on his right hip in a military holster, then slipped into the Beretta 93-R's shoulder rig. From inside the Stealth, he got a couple bandoleers of rounds for the Neostead, then a sheath for the shotgun that ran down his back. Grenades were stashed in the combat webbing he wore. He took up a M-16/M-203 assault rifle-grenade launcher for his lead weapon.

Minutes later, Ayshe joined him.

"Is your grandmother all right?" Bolan asked.

Ayshe nodded curtly.

"What happened?"

"Nothing." Ayshe headed for the small barn that housed the boat—a Cajun-style pirogue—and a trailer. She'd already pulled her grandmother's ancient pickup to the doors. Opening the barn door, she went inside and attempted to fit the trailer to the hitch on the back of the truck.

"Are you going to help me?" Ayshe panted.

"Not until you tell me what's going on," Bolan said.

"It's none of your business." She let the trailer drop with a thump.

"I think it might be."

"Dammit, Fox! You asked for my help. Let's just get this show on the road."

"I needed directions," Bolan said. "I can make it on my own from here." He made no move to help her with the pirogue.

"Maybe you can. But what if something goes wrong and you get lost in the bayous? How many more people are going to die as a result? I'm not prepared to live with that. You're the best chance since the Carrion Killings began to put an end to this." She paused. "If you try leaving me here, I'll drive straight to Lockspur and tell him everything. With helicopters, we can get there before you do."

"And lose the advantage of surprise."

"I'll do it," Ayshe threatened.

"You'll have to walk out of here, then," Bolan assured her. "Because I won't leave either of these vehicles in working order."

"Dammit, Fox, let it go."

"No."

Abruptly, Ayshe started to laugh, but it held a note of hysteria. "You want to know what the problem is? Fine!" She took a deep breath. "Do you believe in superstitions?"

"Like what?"

"That voodoo can raise the dead from the ground and make them walk? That ghosts haunt homes and graveyards? That my grandmother can sometimes foretell the future?"

Ayshe smoothed the hair from her face. "She had a vision in the house. I've seen her have them before. But this one was so powerful that it made her sick when it came. She told me that she saw these people were going to try to kill me sometime tonight."

"Then you're staying here," Bolan said.

"That won't help. If her vision's true, they'll kill me while I'm with you, or while I'm anywhere else. If I try to escape them by running away, leaving you wandering out there in those swamps, I could run straight into the guy I'm supposed to be shot by. Now where do you suppose I'm going to be safest—running, or staying with you?"

Bolan walked back to the car and took two body armor vests from the trunk. He gave one to Ayshe, then looked at her grandmother, who'd come to stand in the doorway of the house. "I'm going to bring her back to you. That's a promise."

The old woman nodded, watching them as they hooked up the boat trailer. Ayshe slid behind the wheel of the truck. They drove away from the clearing, following a narrow, bumpy road.

Bolan didn't try to make conversation. He mentally prepared himself for the coming confrontation and left Ayshe to her own thoughts.

**9**

"Easy."

Mack Bolan heard the voices and silently slipped his oar out of the black water of the bayou.

Ayshe knelt in the forward part of the pirogue. She, too, held her oar in the boat so that it didn't drip water into the bayou. She wore the body armor and carried her Glock in shoulder leather.

Bolan thought he detected the faint gleam of lights in the distance to the east. He pointed in that direction.

Ayshe nodded and dipped her oar back into the sluggish water, bringing them about.

Bolan poled from the rear, and they made contact with the bank. Marisa quickly secured the pirogue to a willow tree whose branches hid the boat. Bolan hoisted his gear and stepped out.

"Are you sure you won't wait here?" he asked Ayshe.

"No, thanks. I haven't come this far to sit in the bleachers." Her determined tone told Bolan she wasn't going to change her mind.

"Lead or follow?" Bolan asked.

"Lead. If you have problems with all that extra bulk you're carrying, let me know." She took off at a brisk pace, expertly working her way through the dense underbrush.

Bolan kept up with her without strain. It began to rain again, blunting the distant glow of lights.

They crested a levee, and Bolan took out his night glasses from his chest pack.

Below them was a clearing. A steep, wood-shingled roof at least thirty feet square had been constructed using the surrounding trees as supports. A number of oil lanterns hung from the roof. There were no walls, and in the open space below, about forty men were gathered. Bolan could see that all of them were armed, either with rifles or side arms. Most of them were dark-skinned, and so it was easier for him to pick out Madigan and Kaliope in the throng.

A ceremony was in progress, and the beat of the drums echoed the sounds of thunder. A potbellied man with a graying fringe of hair around his head and dressed in white cotton pants whirled and danced in the center of the ring of figures.

"That's Papa Glapion," Ayshe whispered.

Bolan had guessed as much. As he watched, Glapion stopped dancing and started to chant. He then bent down and blew white dust into the face of a woman who lay bound on the muddy ground. The drums continued to beat, but now faster and louder.

Bolan and Ayshe watched as the victim's ropes were cut. She lay on the ground, unmoving. Two men separated from the crowd and grabbed the woman's feet and shoulders. They carried her out from under the roof and began to immerse her in the shallow water of a bayou finger.

"Symbolic burial," Ayshe said.

"They're going to kill her," Bolan growled. He pulled out the M-16 and sighted along the barrel. The night scope was almost unusable with the rain.

Bolan knew that if he fired before he could be sure of his targets, he might succeed in saving the woman only for a few brief minutes more, and jeopardize the lives of any of the *bokor*'s other victims. He pushed himself to his feet and started carefully down the incline, staying behind the brush.

Ayshe fell in close behind him, the Glock primed in her fists.

By now, the two men had hauled the woman out of the water and had placed her on the ground again. Then Glapion called to her, his voice harsh and insistent. The woman rose to her feet and stood swaying. At Glapion's direction, she walked over to stand beneath two oak trees west of the roof. It took Bolan a few seconds to realize that other figures were already there, but they'd been so still that he'd missed seeing them in the rain and the darkness.

"My God," Ayshe said softly. "My grandmother said this was the place where men came and had their souls stripped from them. But I thought it was just stories told to frighten children."

"It's the drugs," Bolan said, though that knowledge didn't blunt what he was seeing. Kurtzman had explained it to him during one of their earlier conversations. The existence of zombies had been documented by scientists and researchers. All their findings had agreed that the victims became trapped in an autistic-like state by the *bokor*'s drugs and by social and religious rituals and indoctrination. A return to normality—if it could be achieved—often took months of psychiatric care and counseling.

"I know," Ayshe said. "I keep telling myself that, but it's hard to believe it."

The drums continued to throb. The dancing started again as another victim was chosen.

Bolan rose out of the brush. He spotted a guard behind a large oak tree, a .30-.30 canted across his chest. He signaled to Ayshe to take cover then unleathered the silenced Beretta.

The guy had his eyes fixed on the voodoo ceremony, but some sense had to have warned him, because he started to turn, his weapon raised. The Executioner tightened his finger on the trigger and sent a 9 mm parabellum round through the man's brain. The flash-hider swallowed the muzzle glare.

The man dropped silently into the brush, and Bolan knew he was beyond even a *bokor*'s abilities to make him rise again. He continued on, stopping less than thirty feet from the *hounfour.*

Glapion was leaning over his next victim. Bolan raised the assault rifle to his shoulder and slid his finger through the trigger guard of the M-203. The grenade launcher was chambered with a high-explosive round that would guarantee confusion. He aimed for the knot of Glapion's men farthest from the prisoners, then moved slightly behind them. He pulled the trigger.

The 40 mm HE round sailed true, slamming into a tree behind the men. The explosion was deafening. The blast toppled the tree, and it burst into flames. Bright light speared the night.

Switching to select fire on his M-16, the Executioner managed to score four lethal shots before return fire drove him to cover. He scrambled behind an oak tree and watched as Glapion and his followers scattered. As he reloaded the M-203 with an antipersonnel round, he searched for Madigan and Kaliope. Neither was visible.

He fired the grenade at a small knot of men who'd almost vectored in on his position. The

40 mm warhead hit them in their midst, blasting them in all directions.

A bullet scored the tree bark beside Bolan's face, driving slivers into his cheek.

Tracking the shooter, he dropped the assault rifle's sights over the guy's heart and sprayed a tight triburst into the gunner, putting him down. He flicked the fire selector on the M-16 to full-auto and ripped through the rest of the clip, shooting into the oil lanterns suspended from the roof over Glapion's people. The oil caught fire, and lanterns fell.

Men wreathed in flames burst from the *hounfour* and ran screaming into the forest.

The warrior plunged back into the brush. He dropped the empty clip and was reaching for another one when he sensed movement to his left.

He ducked, at the same time grabbing the Neostead from the over-the-shoulder rig. The shotgun bucked against his palm as he sprayed the brush around him.

The pellets caught the gunner below the waist, blowing his legs out from under him and sending him crashing facefirst into the mud.

Bolan finished reloading the assault rifle. Guns were now going off all around him and voices screamed orders to one another. He realized he had no idea where Ayshe was. Her grandmother's warning loomed in his mind.

Then the sound of helicopter blades beating the air reached him.

Bolan moved on, heading for the place he'd last seen Madigan and Kaliope.

"GET THAT CHOPPER down here!" Arne Madigan barked into his walkie-talkie. "Now!" He took cover behind a tree, the Detonics Scoremaster in his hand.

"So what do you think of Special Agent Fox now?" Kaliope asked, a smile twisting her mud-streaked face.

"I want him dead," Madigan said. He looked up at the night sky, his eyes screwed up against the rain.

The chopper's lights shone uneven cones through the rain, tracking across the ground. Madigan's walkie-talkie buzzed. "I need a landing strip," the pilot said.

Madigan pointed to the people Glapion had worked his black magic on. "Get those people Glapion worked on to the landing strip," Madigan said to Kaliope. "I'll see to the landing lights."

The woman nodded. "You know that'll bring Fox right to us."

"Yeah, so get moving." Madigan plunged into the forest, following a narrow trail he'd mapped out earlier. A shadow loomed in front of him.

He brought the Scoremaster around and rapidly fired three times. The figure fell. As he stepped over the dead man, Madigan saw it was one of Glapion's minions. But at this point, it made no difference to him.

Minutes later he reached the landing strip and located the circuit breaker. He flipped the switch and the lights flooded the area with an incandescent glare.

A file of shambling men and women emerged from the treed area. Kaliope and four men herded the figures ahead of them like a bunch of cattle, pushing them on and shouting orders.

Dull-brained, with their reflexes shot, the zombies reached the landing strip. For Madigan, they represented nothing more than body parts that awaited harvesting.

The helicopter hovered overhead, then began its descent, the rotors whipping up mud and water. Seconds later, it was on the ground.

Madigan grabbed a woman and hustled her into the aircraft's cargo area. Kaliope and the others brought the rest of them, packing them in like sardines.

The organ dealer went forward to the copilot's seat while Kaliope manned the .50-caliber door gun mounted on a swing arm.

"Get us up," Madigan ordered the pilot. He stared through the rain-flecked Plexiglas, wondering where the FBI agent might be. He kept the Detonics tight in his fist, and one foot braced against the door.

The rotors began to gain speed.

As SOON AS SHE SAW the helicopter begin to drop, Ayshe started toward the glowing pool of light in the distance.

The chopper was just above the tree line, descending steadily. She broke into a run, wet branches slapping at her face. Only a second before she found the trail, the helicopter disappeared behind the trees. Another turn took her to within fifty yards of the chopper. She was in time to see the blond-haired woman slip into the doorgunner's rigging. From Fox's briefing, Ayshe knew the woman had to be Kaliope.

The helicopter started to lift slowly, mud dripping from its skids.

"No!" Ayshe screamed, as much as in despair for the prisoners as in frustration. She ran toward the helicopter, the Glock raised in both her hands. She started firing as fast as she could, aiming for the aircraft's rear rotor. With it gone, she knew the pilot wouldn't dare take off.

The deep basso cracking of the machine gun filled her ears, and something hit her in the center of the chest, lifting her off her feet. The Glock flew from her hands. She was dimly aware that she'd hit the ground and was lying in a pool of mud. Then everything went black.

AUTOFIRE RAKED the branches only inches above Mack Bolan's head. He dived for cover, then stripped an antipersonnel grenade from his webbing. Slipping the pin, he tossed the grenade.

The explosion blew two men from hiding, and one shot from the Executioner's M-16 put down the survivor.

On his feet again, Bolan tracked the helicopter as it started to lift into the sky.

Slinging the M-16, the warrior scrambled up into the leafy boughs of a big oak tree that he judged would give him a generous field of fire. The bark scraped his palms, as he pulled himself into position.

He unlimbered his assault rifle. He could identify a half-dozen targets, but the helicopter was gone and there was no sign of Ayshe. With his rifle to his shoulder, and balanced against the bole of the tree for maximum support and protection, the Executioner worked from right to left, pairing the shots as he worked his way through the magazine. When the pop-pop of the M-16 died away, eight men had been taken out of the battle zone.

Autofire from the *hounfour* blasted into the tree.

Fixing the gunner's position in his mind, Bolan squeezed the grenade launcher's trigger. The warhead rocketed across the distance and smacked into a tree supporting the roof. The roof collapsed, covering the gunner.

Bolan slithered down the tree and hit the ground running. He'd met Glapion's forces, and he'd served notice on the butchers behind the organ harvesting. But there were still other targets he had to get his hands on, as well as find Ayshe. Only then could they get the hell out of the area.

He backed around the *hounfour*. Movement ahead of him caught his attention. Despite the rain and the darkness, he recognized Papa Glapion.

Bolan trailed the man and began to close in. He called out. "Glapion!"

The *bokor* looked over his shoulder and saw Bolan. He redoubled his efforts to flee, jogging left.

The soldier followed, shoving his way through the brush and coming into a clearing. Less than twenty feet away, the *bokor* had stopped in the middle of a small cemetery that contained a few tombstones.

"Do you know who I am?" Glapion demanded, facing Bolan.

"Yeah," the Executioner said.

"Then you know the power I wield."

"I know you chose a good place to die," Bolan replied.

"Death holds no fear for me. *I* control death." He pulled a knife from his belt, then he began to chant, raising his voice until the air seemed to vibrate.

Suddenly the earth in front of the gravestones began to shift, and four figures crawled out. They were hollow-eyed, their clothes mud-streaked. All four brandished pistols.

Bolan's mind reeled. There was no way he believed in the supernatural. The only rational explanation he could come up with was that the *bokor* sometimes buried people he'd turned into zombies with his drugs, providing them with breathing tubes or openings. He'd then call them up later with his chanting, for effect.

"Leave," Glapion said, "and I'll let you live."

Bolan switched his gaze back to the *bokor*. "I don't think so."

"Fool!" Glapion barked.

"Kill him!" he ordered his victims.

The zombies started to shuffle forward, their weapons raised. They never had a chance against the Executioner. He whipped the M-16 around in short bursts, knocking his targets back, never to rise again.

The assault rifle was empty when Glapion screamed wildly and rushed at Bolan with his knife poised.

The Executioner shifted the M-16 to his other hand and drew the Desert Eagle. The .44

bucked against his palm and a 240-grain hollowpoint hit the *bokor* in the center of his face.

Glapion twisted backward and hit the ground.

Bolan tossed the charm Liliane had given him onto the corpse as a final gesture. He moved back into the forest, heading for the landing strip, reasoning that that was where Ayshe would have headed.

When he found her, she was lying beside the trail. Her body armor had stopped a slug, but he noticed that she wasn't breathing.

He dragged her into the safety of the brush and started CPR, praying he wasn't too late.

**10**

Marie Desermeaux waited on the bank of the bayou. She wore an ancient yellow slicker that had seen her through thirty-eight hurricane seasons. It had taken her almost two hours to find the spot where her granddaughter and the big man had left the truck and put into the water with the pirogue.

With the rain still falling, she didn't hear the steady slip of the pirogue's oar through the water, nor know it was there until she was able to separate its shadow from the other shadows along the bayou.

She got up stiffly from where she sat on the bank and walked toward the boat.

The FBI man was in the back, paddling smoothly. Her granddaughter lay prone under a blanket she'd packed along the bottom of the pirogue. The man brought the craft into the bank, then got out and dragged it ashore.

Desermeaux knelt and pulled the blanket back. She pressed her hand to her granddaughter's cold cheek. The old woman's eyes filled with tears. Then she felt the thin, warm streams of air from Ayshe's nostrils.

She looked up at the big man. "She's alive."

"Yeah," Bolan replied. He slid his weapons over his shoulder, then gathered the woman in his arms. "I think she's going to be fine." He carried her to the truck, holding her close to keep the rain from falling on her.

"What happened?" Desermeaux asked, helping with the truck door.

Bolan placed Ayshe gently inside. "She was shot with a high-caliber machine gun. Her vest stopped the round, but the impact stopped her heart. Luckily I got there within a couple minutes and got her heart restarted with CPR."

"She was dead?"

"Technically."

"Good," she said and smiled. She could tell that the man was puzzled. "If Marisa was technically dead, then she won't have to go through anything more tonight," she explained. "My visions always come true." She got into the truck, her granddaughter's head resting against her shoulder.

After securing the pirogue, Bolan slid behind the wheel.

"It's not over yet, is it?" Desermeaux asked.

"It is for Marisa," he said.

"But not for you?"

"No."

They rode in silence for a little way. Desermeaux said, "Thank you for bringing her home."

"Your granddaughter's a hell of a woman."

"I know." Desermeaux replied, as she gently smoothed back Ayshe's hair.

"THERE'S AN OUTFIT at New Orleans International Airport," Eduard Hamlin told Bolan, "called Executive Transport. They specialize in flying oil-field management all over the world. They also have a helicopter section that makes regular runs to and from the Gulf area. One of my people called me when they saw that an emergency flight plan was filed by one of the pilots just after that guy Dreyser was dealt with in the hospital yesterday. I've got a couple guys on it now. If I find out anything more, you'll know."

"I'll check it out," Bolan said. "If I don't get something soon, the only thing I'll have on my plate will be to bring you more grief.'' He punched the End button on the cellular phone.

The big man sat in the Stealth in front of the Desermeaux home. The rain still hadn't let up. He'd made sure Ayshe was doing okay. She had come to twice, Desermeaux had said, but had gone back to sleep almost immediately. Both times she'd appeared lucid and remembered what had happened.

Bolan took a sip of the coffee the old woman had fixed for him, then punched in the number for Stony Man Farm. Kurtzman was still catching at the keyboard, and he gave the cybernetics specialist the courier service's name.

Blearily Bolan glanced at the car's clock. Fatigue was starting to set in bone-deep. He closed his eyes.

When Kurtzman called back, Bolan caught it on the first ring.

''Got it,'' Kurtzman said, a note of triumph in his voice. ''Executive Courier has been in business since the late sixties, which is one of the reasons I didn't look at them initially, seeing as we were going for new companies. Also, they primarily cater to the oil-and-gas industry. It's a privately owned company and has changed hands only twice, the second time in September of last year."

"Madigan?" Bolan asked.

"Yeah. He did some fancy footwork with the ownership papers, most of it quite legal. But the signature at the bottom of the licensing is that of Carlton Quincy, one of the aliases Madigan used that the Hong Kong people were investigating."

Bolan brought up the computer. "Can you fax me a printout of the particulars?"

"Sure." In a moment, paper started spooling out of the printer.

The soldier's mind was working furiously. "The chances are slim that Madigan's operating the organ harvests out of the airport warehouses."

"I agree. Inspections, plus the daily traffic through the airport, would make that impossible."

"Are there any other buildings that have been purchased or leased under the name of Carlton Quincy?"

"Nope. But the guy does have a lease on a jack-up barge out in the Gulf, about an hour's flight from New Orleans."

"Executive Courier has regular helicopter runs to and from the Gulf," Bolan said, remembering his earlier conversation with Hamlin.

"Right. It's a good cover, Striker. You've got to hand it to the guy, he's definitely a solid strategist."

"What can you give me on the barge?"

"Everything you want."

"Let me have it."

Paper started spilling out of the printer, from ownership documents to diagrams detailing the security systems on the barge. Bolan knew that once he'd reviewed the information, he'd have a good idea of how he meant to handle the situation.

He broke the connection to Stony Man Farm, separated the papers into two piles and got out of the car. He knocked on Desermeaux's front door.

The old woman answered.

"I've got to leave," he said. "But I wanted Marisa to have these. He handed her one stack of papers. "They pretty much document her case for her. But wait a few hours before you give them to her because it could make things difficult for me."

Desermeaux took his hand for a moment and gazed up at him. "I tried to see what the future might hold for you. I saw nothing, but I could sense death all around you. I don't know if it was because you're so close to your own death, or because you walk so near to death that you can no longer be separated from it."

"Both, maybe," the Executioner said. "I've lived with that for a long time, and I don't have an answer either. Tell Marisa goodbye for me." He turned and headed for his car. Kurtzman would have a helicopter waiting for Special Agent Travis Fox at New Orleans International Airport by the time he got there. He needed to reach the barge by dawn.

"THEY'RE BEGINNING to prep the first one," Winston Chen said.

Arne Madigan looked up from the computer in his office on the barge. "Good." He got up from his chair and joined Chen at the viewing window overlooking the OR. The first of Glapion's zombies was on the table.

"Twelve organ removals in one day," Chen said happily. "There's never been a cash crop like this. If we could do this every day for just one month, we could retire.

"You and I know there's plenty of business out there," Chen went on. "That organ-sharing network alone has over twenty thousand people on their list needing organs. A good percentage of those have means to leverage some buying power, even at our prices. And that list is going to increase."

"A two-week hiatus isn't going to hurt either of us," Madigan said.

Chen sighed. "No, I suppose not. But now that Glapion's involved and more people are readily accessible to us for tissue matches, it seems we could gear up production."

"And we will," Madigan assured him. He ushered the doctor to the door. "Your patients are waiting for you."

Kaliope, who had been sitting on a corner of his desk, picked up the remote control that also linked the television to the outside security cameras mounted around the jack-up barge. She flicked through the different angles they covered, from the sea horizon and the coastline, to the slate-gray sky.

"If he knew where we were," Madigan said, "he'd be here by now."

"Maybe," Kaliope replied. "He worries you, doesn't he?"

"No more than anyone else."

"What do you suppose happened to the *bokor?*"

"I'd like to think he's alive and that the FBI agent is dead."

Madigan stared out at the sea, then turned to walk to the piano and began to finger the keys. "After the bank accounts have been settled," he said over his shoulder, "why don't you let me take you to Rio? There's a number of pursuits we can get involved in there to whet even your appetites."

"Fine," she said.

With a feeling that things were looking up, Madigan went back to his computer.

MACK BOLAN PILOTED the SEAL Swimmer Delivery Vehicle easily through the Gulf waters. The SDV Mk 9 was designed to carry two divers. Its built-in oxygen tanks could last for hours. For his mission, Bolan had ordered it dropped from the military helicopter Kurtzman had arranged. Run through Brognola's Sensitive Operations Group contacts, no questions had been asked.

He'd cruised under water for the better part of forty minutes to reach the jack-up barge, running between ten and twenty feet below the surface. A half mile from the derrick he'd gone deeper, taking the SDV down to forty feet so it wouldn't be seen by any sentries posted on the barge.

He cut the power and drifted in between the legs of the barge's jacket. Switching from the SDV's oxygen supply to his own rebreather unit, he secured the craft to a leg. Then, armed with his waterproof equipment bag, he swam slowly to the surface.

The barge deck towered thirty-five feet above him. He didn't see any guards, but he took careful note of where the security cameras were mounted, with dual housings that signified infrared capabilities.

Climbing onto one of the jacket legs where the security cameras couldn't pick him up, Bolan stripped off his wet suit, revealing the combat blacksuit he wore underneath. He pulled on a pair of running shoes from his equipment bag, then sheathed the Desert Eagle on his hip and the Beretta 93-R in a shoulder rig. Grenades and extra magazines for the pistols and for the Heckler & Koch MP-5 machine pistol he carried were secured around his body in the military webbing. For his lead weapon, he'd selected the M-16/M-203 combo that had seen him through his last firefight. His body armor had pockets that held additional munitions.

He glanced up the length of the barge's legs and saw a set of railings positioned roughly every twenty feet. From his equipment bag, he uncoiled a collapsible grappling hook on a nylon cord and cast it upward, hooking his target on the first try. He climbed to the first railing, then held on while he cast again.

In minutes he'd made the deck level on the side that held the helipad. The octagon stuck out from the platform and two guards patrolled it. Making sure that neither the guards nor the cameras picked him up, Bolan mined the helipad and hooked the remote control for the detonators to the body armor on his chest.

Following the layout of the barge he'd memorized, he then made his way down to the preproduction plant for processing the crude oil. He completed some more demolitions work designed to take advantage of the volatile nature of the oil-refinery equipment. Another ten minutes was spent with charges designed to sever the flare arm next to the deck railing.

He completed his preparations only two minutes after Brognola was supposed to have communicated with the Coast Guard concerning the organ harvesting ring on the jack-up barge. Four minutes later, he was once more atop the refinery station.

He slipped the M-16/M-203 combo from his shoulder while he took up a position behind the low wall at the top of the production plant.

Whirling the grappling hook over his head, he made the cast to what he knew was the top of the first-floor railing of the living quarters. Its rooftop was a good six feet lower than his present position, so that the cord slanted after he'd tied it off. The cord ran behind two yellow storage silos and wasn't clearly visible.

He knew from his earlier recon when he'd set his explosives that Madigan's probable location was the living quarters' second floor. The operating room, therefore, had to be located somewhere on the first floor. From his present position, he could see plate-glass windows overlooking the barge deck and the Gulf waters.

He took a pair of fingerless black gloves from his chest pack and pulled them on. Hefting the M-16, he laid out six 40 mm smoke grenades on the railing, then chambered the first one.

Looking through the rifle's telescopic sights, he laid the cross hairs over the heart of an armed guard standing on the observation platform nearest him. Two more guards were there as well. He squeezed the trigger.

The rifle bucked as the man collapsed. Bolan moved on, seeking his targets, knowing he had only a second or two of confusion and sluggish reflexes on his side. He fired twice more, making them both head shots and putting the men down.

Shifting to the M-203, he aimed at the barge's metal deck and pulled the trigger. He reloaded, working the action of the grenade launcher until he'd hit the four cardinal points of the compass he'd marked on the deck in his mind, then added two in the center.

A fog of red smoke billowed over the barge as Klaxons started blaring out a warning that was already too late.

Return fire struck the railing over Bolan's position. He ducked and moved down, away from the secured cord that was his escape route. He slipped the remote-control detonator from his armor and keyed in the sequence that set off the charges on the flare arm.

The detonation of the C-4 caused the barge to shiver, then the metal structure twisted violently and sheared away from the deck. The gas by-product that had been directed safely away from the barge to be burned off suddenly flared to new life and washed over a group of guards standing nearby. Some of them were burned to death where they stood while others threw themselves into the sea.

Leaning into the M-16, the Executioner accounted for five more men before he had to take cover from their return fire.

"Get that bastard!" a man's voice blasted from the PA system mounted on the central derrick.

Bolan thumbed an HE round into the M-203's breach and snapped it closed. He fired the 40 mm warhead at the PA speakers, blowing them to smithereens. A glance over the side of the railing showed him that the deckhands were converging on the production facility. He picked out five targets and managed to put three of them down before he was driven to ground. Some of the deckhands were already racing up the metal stairs that ran up one side of the structure.

Slinging the rifle over his shoulder, the warrior sprinted to the cord he'd tied at the building's edge. Gripping it in his gloved hands, he threw himself over. The angle of the rope sped him along. The gloves grew warm, then his feet thudded against the concrete wall of the living quarters.

He swung himself up and over the railing as bullets cracked into the building's side. Coming up on one knee, Bolan keyed in the sequence that would detonate the charges on the production facility.

Fueled by the flammable liquids contained in the building, the explosion caused the barge to shudder on its moorings. The fuel-air combination formed fiery clouds atop the building that roiled orange and black. The flames and smoke rained death on the deckhands. The building was soon reduced to a gutted shell, while great pools of flame fed by the spilled liquid flowed across the deck, killing and injuring still others.

Bolan pushed himself up and turned to the large plate-glass window nearest him. He could detect movement on the other side of the glass.

He snatched up the H&K MP-5 and found the trigger. Emptying the clip into the window in a blazing figure eight, he chopped away at the glass. While fragments were still falling, he reloaded the machine pistol, then charged through the empty windowframe.

He took in the room at a glance. A blond-haired woman lay facedown on the floor. There appeared to be no one else in the room.

The Executioner kept the doorways covered as he edged toward the woman. He nudged her with the MP-5's barrel.

She didn't move.

Reaching behind his back, Bolan took hold of a pair of plastic handcuffs and got ready to put them on her. He rolled the woman onto her face, and realized it was Kaliope. He reached down for her hand.

Instead, she kept on rolling, then came up with a fistful of razor-sharp claws that had been hidden between her fingers.

Only the skills honed in years of battle allowed the Executioner to pull back in time to save his eyes. Still, the three blades sliced neatly along his cheek, drawing blood.

She came at him like a tiger, screaming and spitting.

Bolan stood his ground. He blocked her follow-up slash with a sweeping cross block, then backhanded her across the face, hitting her hard enough to lift her from her feet and deposit her a couple yards away.

When she got up, her nose and mouth were bleeding. Bolan held the Desert Eagle in his fist.

"Are you going to shoot me?" she asked, still brandishing the claws.

"If I have to. It's your choice."

"Die or be your prisoner," she said. She licked her bloodied lips. "Do you know how long it's been since a man controlled me physically?"

Bolan didn't reply.

"I swore to myself it would never happen again. The choices I make are mine—no one else's. No matter what the cost."

For a moment the Executioner thought she was going to rush him, forcing him to shoot her. Instead, she turned and threw herself through the plate-glass window that overlooked the OR thirty feet below.

Bolan heard her strike the ground with a sickening thud. Looking down at her sprawled body and the impossible twist of her neck,

Bolan knew that she wouldn't be getting up again.

Exiting through a door on his right, Bolan went down a flight of steps until he reached the OR. The people Glapion had drugged stood in a frightened huddle in one corner of the room.

Two armed men moved out from behind some hospital equipment to get the drop on Bolan.

He cut them down with a pair of short bursts and was through the door and almost on the main deck before their bodies hit the ground. Flames continued to sear the metal about the barge, and clouds of smoke hung dark and oily in the air.

Bolan spotted Madigan streaking for the helipad and gave chase.

At the same time, a trio of gunners emerged from the derrick assembly and cut loose.

Diving to the right, the Executioner rolled out of the path of their gunfire and came up on one knee with the machine pistol braced on top of his thigh. The 9 mm rounds knocked the gunners down.

A yellow helicopter equipped with pontoon floats sat waiting on the helipad, its rotor whirling near liftoff speed.

Madigan was closing in on it fast.

Reaching for the detonator, Bolan keyed in the final sequence. A heartbeat later, the helipad erupted in an explosion that caught the chopper in its deadly embrace, smashing it into fiery pieces that rained over the Gulf waters.

Madigan stumbled to a halt, his pistol clenched in his fist.

The roar and crackle of flames filled the void left by the explosion. Bolan drew the Desert Eagle and walked toward Madigan.

In the distance, coming from the west, a trio of fat-bodied sea helicopters flew toward the barge.

"That's the Coast Guard," Bolan said as he came to a stop.

Madigan looked to where the explosives had ripped the helipad platform, leaving a jagged hole. "It appears I've run out of positions to retreat to."

"Yeah," Bolan said.

"What about Kaliope?" the man asked.

"Dead."

"She was certain you'd fall for her game. Pity it didn't work out that way."

"She gave it her best shot."

"I don't suppose there's a chance I could give myself up and throw myself at the mercy of the court?" Madigan tried.

"No. You've killed too many innocents to walk away from this."

"Then I guess we get to find out who's the better man." His move was like greased lighting as he brought up the gun.

Bolan's move was almost a mirror image of Madigan's. He pointed and squeezed the trigger, unable to differentiate the sound of his round going off from the other man's. Madigan's bullet burned the warrior's neck as it passed by him. The Executioner's round caught the man between the eyes and knocked him over the jagged edge of what had been part of the helipad.

By the time Bolan reached the deck's ripped perimeter, Madigan was floating facedown in the water. The New Orleans police and the Coast Guard would clear up whatever mystery remained of the organ-harvesting operation. Bolan knew his part in it would never come to light, except under his Agent Fox cover. Brognola would see to that.

But he couldn't afford to be caught on the barge. He leaped off the deck into the Gulf, the salt water stinging his wounds. By the time the first helicopter was hovering over the derrick, he'd retrieved his rebreather and wet suit, and was swimming for the SDV. He headed back the way he'd come.

Advances in medical science and technology offered new hope, but Bolan knew that men like Madigan would find ways to corrupt that hope and twist it into a greed that knew no bounds. Every day brought the future closer, and the Executioner was determined to fight to keep it from being a dark one.

**With terror at home and a nuclear nightmare, Stony Man is the President's last hope**

# STONY MAN™ 24
## BIRD OF PREY

At Stony Man Farm in Virginia, world trouble spots are monitored around the clock. And when watch-and-wait tactics aren't enough, the elite field teams go behind the lines—and beyond the law.

Available in September at your favorite retail outlet.

**Don't miss out on the action in these titles featuring
THE EXECUTIONER®, and STONY MAN™!**

SuperBolan

| #61445 | SHOWDOWN | $4.99 U.S. | ☐ |
| | | $5.50 CAN. | ☐ |
| #61446 | PRECISION KILL | $4.99 U.S. | ☐ |
| | | $5.50 CAN. | ☐ |
| #61447 | JUNGLE LAW | $4.99 U.S. | ☐ |
| | | $5.50 CAN. | ☐ |
| #61448 | DEAD CENTER | $5.50 U.S. | ☐ |
| | | $6.50 CAN. | ☐ |

Stony Man™

| #61904 | TERMS OF SURVIVAL | $4.99 U.S. | ☐ |
| | | $5.50 CAN. | ☐ |
| #61905 | SATAN'S THRUST | $4.99 U.S. | ☐ |
| | | $5.50 CAN. | ☐ |
| #61906 | SUNFLASH | $5.50 U.S. | ☐ |
| | | $6.50 CAN. | ☐ |
| #61907 | THE PERISHING GAME | $5.50 U.S. | ☐ |
| | | $6.50 CAN. | ☐ |

(limited quantities available on certain titles)

| TOTAL AMOUNT | $ |
| POSTAGE & HANDLING | $ |
| ($1.00 for one book, 50¢ for each additional) | |
| APPLICABLE TAXES* | $_____ |
| TOTAL PAYABLE | $_____ |
| (check or money order—please do not send cash) | |

To order, complete this form and send it, along with a check or money order for the total above, payable to Gold Eagle Books, to: **In the U.S.:** 3010 Walden Avenue, P.O. Box 9077, Buffalo, NY 14269-9077; **In Canada:** P.O. Box 636, Fort Erie, Ontario, L2A 5X3.

Name:_____

Address:_____ City:_____

State/Prov.:_____ Zip/Postal Code: _____

*New York residents remit applicable sales taxes.
Canadian residents remit applicable GST and provincial taxes.

GEBACK15A

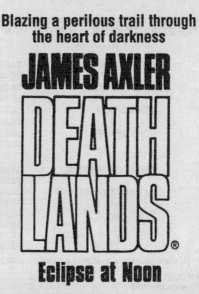

**Don't miss out on the action in these titles featuring
THE EXECUTIONER®, and STONY MAN™!**

The Red Dragon Trilogy

| | | | |
|---|---|---|---|
| #64210 | FIRE LASH | $3.75 U.S.<br>$4.25 CAN. | ☐<br>☐ |
| #64211 | STEEL CLAWS | $3.75 U.S.<br>$4.25 CAN. | ☐<br>☐ |
| #64212 | RIDE THE BEAST | $3.75 U.S.<br>$4.25 CAN. | ☐<br>☐ |

The Executioner®

| | | | |
|---|---|---|---|
| #64204 | RESCUE RUN | $3.50 U.S.<br>$3.99 CAN. | ☐<br>☐ |
| #64205 | HELL ROAD | $3.50 U.S.<br>$3.99 CAN. | ☐<br>☐ |
| #64206 | HUNTING CRY | $3.75 U.S.<br>$4.25 CAN. | ☐<br>☐ |
| #64207 | FREEDOM STRIKE | $3.75 U.S.<br>$4.25 CAN. | ☐<br>☐ |
| #64208 | DEATH WHISPER | $3.75 U.S.<br>$4.25 CAN. | ☐<br>☐ |
| #64209 | ASIAN CRUCIBLE | $3.75 U.S.<br>$4.25 CAN. | ☐<br>☐ |

**(limited quantities available on certain titles)**

| | |
|---|---|
| **TOTAL AMOUNT** | $ |
| **POSTAGE & HANDLING** | $ |
| ($1.00 for one book, 50¢ for each additional) | |
| **APPLICABLE TAXES*** | $_____ |
| **TOTAL PAYABLE** | $_____ |
| (check or money order—please do not send cash) | |

To order, complete this form and send it, along with a check or money order for the total above, payable to Gold Eagle Books, to: **In the U.S.:** 3010 Walden Avenue, P.O. Box 9077, Buffalo, NY 14269-9077; **In Canada:** P.O. Box 636, Fort Erie, Ontario, L2A 5X3.

Name:_____

Address:_____ City:_____

State/Prov.:_____ Zip/Postal Code: _____

*New York residents remit applicable sales taxes.
Canadian residents remit applicable GST and provincial taxes.

GEBACK15